to Dr. t,,,,...,

You Are

A GIFT OF LOVE

to your

Patients

Nancy Walton Fricke

Nancy

IN APPRECIATION

Thanks for support and encouragement: Virginia Mauch, Alisa and Matthew Johnson, Lupe Castro, Thelma La Motte, my friends at Creekside Christian Church in Elk Grove, the EGSC Writers Group and my friends in Bob/Norma Lane's Bible Study.

Heartfelt thanks to Araceli Mendoza who cuts my hair, scrubs my floors and cures my computer ills. A big thanks to Mirla Mendoza and Penny Clark for formatting and getting "A Gift Of Love" ready for publication.

DEDICATION

"A Gift of Love "is fiction, and is dedicated to my four grandsons: Jason, Joshua, Matthew and Stephen and to my children: Susan, Mark, Jane and Janet and in memory of their father, George and our son, Georgie, both deceased.

TABLE OF CONTENTS

Aristotle said, "An unexamined life is a life not worth living." After both spouses had died, T.J. and Jane were to connect again. Jane had given up her chemo cancer treatments and T.J.'s cancer was now in his blood. For eighteen months, God gave them time to examine their lives and the gifts they had given each other. They discussed their faith, their careers of service, laughed together and appreciated each other. They didn't understand why or what was happening but they accepted it as God's "Gift of Love."

COMING OF AGE

Strengthened by a tough childhood in the Great Depression, softened by patriotism, encouraged to have faith and sweetened by love of family and friends, "The Greatest Generation" represented the best of our country.

In the twenties, few people wanted war. The 20th Century had changed the United States. We had been isolationists—raw courage and hard work determined fortune and fate. To the European countries, we seemed uncultured, not third world but a diamond in the rough sort of nation. We were a country of immigrants. We had bountiful natural resources and we were emerging.

World War 1 had been regretted. Soldiers died, some were wounded and others had been gassed in the war. No one wanted to get into another war in Europe. This mood was followed by the undisciplined years of the "Roaring Twenties." People were disobeying the Victorian rules of conduct. Irving Berlin and Cole Porter were sharing their genius with songs like "Make Every Day a Holiday" by Porter and "All Alone" by Al Jolson. "The Thief of Bagdad" played at the movie theater. The average annual income was $2,195 and rent was $18.00 a month. They paid 11 cents a gallon for gas for their new cars that costs $250. "Kiss Me Again" was being sung as the roaring twenties felt like "Happy Days" would never end.

Then the Crash came and the Depression put a shadow over the land. Growing up in this era produced young people who could deal with reality sweeten by hope. They learned to do with what was at hand or use ingenuity in fixing it themselves. Nothing was wasted. Not much was easy. The banks had closed and the savings of the middle class were lost. Jobs disappeared, and people lost their farms.

The country elected a new leader, Franklin Delano Roosevelt, who set about putting some safety nets in place. 1935-1942 WPA (Works Progress Administration) and CCC (Civilian Conversation Corps) helped put many people back to work and yet the country was still in the Depression when Europe went to war. The Japanese attack on Pearl Harbor came and we had no choice. Able men, 18 and older had to register. The lottery for the draft began in Washington, D.C. When your number came up, you were drafted. Many of the young men being drafted were born around 1924 when Calvin College was President and life expectancy was 54.1 years.

The United States was claiming its place in the world as a leader in the movie industry. The movies had a big influence on style and behavior. The passionate love consummated off screen as the romantic soft music set the tone. Most stories were girl meets boy, difficulties kept them in desperate situations and then they overcome these and he proposed, she accepted and they got married. They never lived together without marriage. Some murders ended marriage but few divorces. Clothing customs changed as Clark Gable took off his shirt and revealed no underwear in "It Happened One Night." Cary Grant was sophisticated and had a comedian's coolness. "Braveheart" and "Black Pirate" and many other movies portrayed brave, courageous men who overcame impossible odds. Honor and integrity were favored over fame and fortune.

Single women in the movies were tough as detectives, writers, and career women. They also appeared perfect in face and figure.

Little of this was going on in real life. The leading man was handsome, brave, and strong and always "he could not love the girl so much unless he loved honor more."

Most of the children in the movies were cute, smart and talented. An example was Shirley Temple who could dance, sing and act. She was a box office draw and people would attend movies if she were the feature actress. The movies were innocent since public taste and censors liked them that way.

Stories about the Wild West featured rustlers in black hats and handsome white cowboys in white hats. There was a lot of guitar singing and always a comic sidekick. Often in twin billing was a detective story and a serial. These were particularly popular on Saturday afternoon as matinee tickets were cheaper. Pre-teens spent three or four hours in a trance while watching them. When all of the popcorn was eaten, they could chew on bubble gum. Many teens worked on Saturday during the day and went to the movies on Saturday night. All of this depended on getting the right amount of change for the ticket. As for dates, girls never paid for anything.

Sunday meant church for most people and if they didn't go, someone would visit or call to find out why. The Baptist were "big" on Sunday School with boys' only and girls' only classes. There was an evening service, Wednesday night prayer meeting, and many other groups to join. Boy Scouts and Girl Scouts often met in the church. Dinners and church entertainment furnished the social life.

The developmentally disabled, gays, alcoholics, drug addicts were hidden by the family, if possible. Gentile poverty prevailed as people lost fortunes when the banks collapsed and some lost farms when the droughts came. Pride was prevalent! People did the best they knew how!

So begins our story!

"A GIFT of LOVE" is a fictional account of one couple who grew up in this era. The setting is a typical small industrial town in the South where many of the cotton mills and furniture factories were located. The music, movies, and churches that influenced them were shared by others who lived in cities or on farms. "A Gift of Love" could be a fun, nostalgic read for some and hopefully it contains life lessons for others.

The United States had become a World Power after World War ll. Their industrial and training power out distanced the rest of the world's nations. Before using the atomic bomb, the U.S. had met with Britain and they both agreed that if Japan didn't agree to un-conditionally surrender, that the bomb must be used. Going into Japan would lose many of the Allies' soldiers and the Japanese cities would all have to be taken, killing many civilians. The Potsdam Declaration demanded unconditional surrender or be annihilated. There was no response! August 6, 1945, the first uranium bomb (Little Boy) was released on Hiroshima. No response! The second bomb was plutonium (Big Boy) was released on Nagasaki three days later on August 9. 90,000 to 146,000 people were killed. So began the Atomic Age.

In post war, the Marshall Plan became the U.S.'s best effort to foster world peace. The U.S. helped nations rebuild after a devastating war that had ravished the landscape and crippled the people. The U.S had proved its mettle as an industrial and scientific power and a moral leader with a big heart.

At home, the U.S. had escaped bombing and attacks but they had hard lessons to be learned about integration while also soul searching the disgrace of interning Japanese Americans just because they looked like the enemy. There was much to be learned in this "coming of age" for all of us.

CHAPTER 1
HOLDING HANDS

T.J.'s hand had reached down and touched hers. This was a new excitement she had never felt before. She glanced at him and he smiled, she smiled but little was said as they joined their gang of friends and he walked her home from the Rives Theater. That was Saturday night and she hadn't seen him at the First Baptist Church when she sat in the balcony with her friends. Evelyn had said he was a football star and he didn't seem to have a girlfriend. He lived in the Cotton Mill part of town and went to their high school. He had red hair, and blue eyes, and freckles. She had added that he was real quiet. Evelyn knew everything about school because she was a sophomore and Jane was just a freshman, in school since September. Their mothers had been friends so when they wanted to do something each would say that the other mother had okayed it. Worked most of the time. It was hard to sleep Sunday night since Monday was school, and she might get to see him in the daylight and he might be disappointed.

Jane opened the old green icebox on the back porch and retrieved the glass bottle of milk. She shook it vigorously to mix the cream with the rest of the liquid. Before going into the kitchen, she stood a moment and admired the view of her Blue Ridge

Mountains. She sure wished she could go for a ride and see the fall colors of orange and red that painted the mountains in late October. No luck with that because of gas rationing and even tires were at a premium.

The ice man always brought the huge blocks of ice around the back to the porch ice box. The kitchen had a gas stove and then a wood stove for baking. There was a Frigidaire that was quite old but kept buzzing along. These were all in use by two black women, Carrie and Emma, who took command of the kitchen. They said they liked Jane but she got in their way.

One step up from the kitchen was a long, rectangular room that contained two dining tables, with white table cloths and a carafe of vinegar Sometimes a magnolia blossom floated in a flat vase and always there was sugar, salt and pepper plus a jar of Tabasco and hot peppers. Southerners like to spice up their collard greens and kale. Butter would be there for the biscuits in the morning, corn bread at dinner and hot homemade yeast rolls for supper. Meals were a serious matter.

Jane wasn't thinking of breakfast as Carrie brought her usual oatmeal and stacks of bacon. Her mother, a dietician at the local hospital, believed that a big breakfast fortified the day. When Jane was little, her mother had crumbled bacon on Jane's oatmeal to coax her to eat it. She still liked it that way. Biscuits spread with butter and strawberry jam were washed down with a tall glass of milk. Then, Jane was out the door to meet her day and maybe him.

The house she left was a large, two story white colonial with green shutters framing the windows. Full green hedges bordered the walkway to the street. Jane and her sister, Annie, and parents lived downstairs and the "guests" lived upstairs. The guests were mostly mountain girls who had moved to Turnersville to work in the factories. Besides the cotton mill and furniture factory, there was a new Du Point Plant that mostly made parachutes used in the War. The men had gone to fight and the patriotic thing to do was to go to work making supplies for the war effort. An interesting fact to Jane was that the Japanese and Germans didn't allow women to work in their factories so they were very short of workers.

Walking to school was a social event for Jane. Next door lived Wilma and then they picked up Doris and Dora who lived next to Wilma. They seemed to both talk and listen at the same time. Most of the talk was about what happened over the week end and since they had all been at the movies with Jane, she wanted to talk about HIM. It was a short conversation since Dora was a sophomore and had a silent crush on T.J. She had noticed the handholding and didn't approve. Jane had experienced Dora's sharp tongue before and was not inclined to stir up trouble. Conversation switched to Jane's birthday party and if any boys were invited. They were, but whether they would come or not was another question.

The walk to school was about a mile through downtown Turnersville. They passed Roses' and Penny's then the hospital and the movie theater. The last block was a sprint since they heard the bell calling students in for homeroom. Jane had dressed in her new gold pleated skirt and purple sweater. That summer she had worked at Smart and Thrifty's Dress Shop and this was her first purchase there. Dresses were usually $2.98 but her grandmother made her dresses and of much better quality material and fashion. Time to look for him while pretending not to look.

She spotted Peggy, her best friend, coming to the locker they shared. Peggy wanted to know right away if she had heard from "that boy?" Then they both started looking unobtrusively. Kind of.

"I want to invite him to my birthday party," Jane whispered, "but I'm afraid he will think I am forward. Suppose he doesn't remember me."

"It was just Saturday night, Jane, and you said he held your hand." Peggy was always matter of fact.

"I am not sure what he looks like in the daylight but Evelyn said he had red hair. I think Dora likes him."

"That could be a problem. You know how she is," Peggy warned. Dora and the sophomores controlled Hi-Y and Jane had not been invited to join though Peggy and Wilma had joined.

"Makes it more of a challenge," Jane smiled but she wasn't at all confident. She had never really dated. The gossip was that Dora was experienced. She certainly was pretty with blond naturally curly hair and she was a cheerleader. Jane had brown hair that she rolled up in socks every night. Her eyes were brown but her best feature was a merry sense of humor. Smiles were easy to come by and she was accused of being a Pollyanna. She naturally liked people and they liked her. Sometimes reality brought her down to earth but not for long before she was back to humming along again.

Peggy left for class and there he stood. First she noticed a mischievous smile and eyes that twinkled. He had a football player's physique that bragged of a maroon wool letter sweater. Her heart pounded. Mustn't look too anxious, she said, "Hi."

"HI, yourself. Remember me? I wondered if you wanted to go to another movie this Saturday night?"

"Yes." Why couldn't she think of anything clever to say? "I got to go to class." She ran off in the wrong direction, then turned on her heels past him and sped toward English 101. The rest of the day was amazing!

CHAPTER 2
PIANO LESSONS

Jane walked slowly to Miss Leaner's home studio for piano lesson torture. She definitely was going to quit today. It was a waste of money and everyone's time. She gently kicked the fall leaves that covered the walk entrance to the old red brick two story. The dormer windows had been shuttered for years. No one went upstairs because Miss Leaner quit climbing stairs after her broken hip had mended. She slept in the Sun Parlor and ate in the kitchen. The living room displayed her Baby Grand piano. Her livelihood was provided by the church and piano lesson funds. Grandma paid $5.00 a month for Jane's lessons.

The mammoth front door with a glass inset opened with a push. It was never locked in the daytime so the students could come and go without having their teacher leave her post. Miss Leaner was so thin, her bony fingers were almost skeleton like. Jane called out but there was no answer so she preceded into the living room to deliver her ultimatum. There on the floor lay Miss Leaner in her familiar lavender and lace long sheer gown.

Jane raced to her and tried to lift her head but even Jane could tell she was dead. Jane put her down gently and called her mother.

"Don't leave. I'll call the ambulance," said Mrs. Carter. "Find a shawl and cover her to show respect. I am glad you found her or she might have been there for days, living alone and all." This last sentiment was to be shared and told to her by everyone at the church memorial.

Jane sat on the horsehair maroon love seat. She noticed a gold framed picture of a soldier in a World War 1 uniform. It was on the mantel piece in a place of honor. Inscribed was "All my love, all my life, Robert." Jane was still shaken up by seeing her first dead person but she imagined that this was Miss Leaner's Robert and the reason she was not married and sad all the time. They must have been very much in love. He probably died in the war and Miss Leaner never got over it. Well, she wouldn't be able to ask her about it now.

The ambulance drove up and whisked Miss Leaner away. Jane locked the door as they all left. She hoped someone had a key.

That night she had trouble sleeping. It was her first time of seeing a dead person. Her mother came into the room and sat holding her hand while they talked.

"We are here for a purpose and to do God's will. It was Miss Leaner's time. She had a good long life and loved the Lord. She served the church and added music to the world," Mrs. Carter said.

Jane had a fit of conscience. "I had planned to quit piano lessons today and tell her and Grandmother. You know I never practice. I feel a little guilty that I am relieved that I didn't have to go through that."

Her mother chuckled, "They say something good comes out of everything if you look for it."

Jane smiled. She didn't fall asleep right away. She thought about her little friend, Buddy, in third grade. He was so sweet with big brown eyes and blond curly hair. He had died of diabetes and Jane just didn't understand the concept of death. Her mother had held her hand almost all night until she finally cried herself to sleep.

The next day at school, his desk was empty. At recess, she looked for him to play marbles, then realized he would never be there again. There was a heavy feeling in *her chest that day. Miss Leaner's death was different but she would never be there again either.*

The funeral was Friday afternoon and since Jane was a celebrity of sorts, her mother let her miss school. It was at the First Baptist Church, the big downtown church that Jane had attended since she was in Cradle Roll class. Rev. McCabe preached a long memorial. An older woman who had been a student of Miss Leaner's played the organ while a lady of similar age and ample figure, sang high soprano. They said they wanted to honor their former mentor who was a woman of God. Lots of other people said nice things while they enjoyed small sandwiches, cake and punch in the basement. Everyone told Jane how glad they were that she had found Miss Leaner since she lived alone. Jane still felt a little guilty since she was very happy that she didn't have to take piano lessons anymore. Her grandmother said that she was sorry about Miss Leaner's death but now they would try voice lessons.

Saturday was a beautiful fall day…sweater weather. Jane had an agreement with the manager of Smart and Thrifty that she would not work on Game Day. Jane loved the excitement of a parade and the marching band. The game began at two in the afternoon but she and Peggy were in their seats by one since none of the seats were reserved and she wanted to see every play. T.J. played the position of center and wore number 51. This was the first time she had a special player to root for.

As the starting gun of the 1942 season, they were playing football against Pulaski High School. Their team was expected to win and they did. The score was 35 to 21 and to Jane and Peggy that provided a lot of screaming time. T.J. intercepted a football pass and as he ran, someone tore his jersey. His shirt was almost torn off of him as he made the touchdown. The crowd roared and cheered and even some of the men stood up and clapped. High school football was serious business in Turnersville, Southwestern Virginia.

Jane could hardly eat supper and it was a favorite. The pork chops were coated with seasoned flour and then fried in lard. Tonight they had apple sauce, slaw, scalloped potatoes, and rolls. Dessert was banana pudding. Jane ate the banana pudding and drank her ice tea. Everyone knew she had a date so nothing was said about her not cleaning her plate.

The doorbell rang and Mary Carter insisted that she was the one to welcome the guest. He politely introduced himself as T.J. Jennings. He looked so handsome in a blue sports coat.

Jane came quickly and had no intention of being coy. She welcomed T.J. with a big smile and said, "You were terrific today." Immediately, he felt comfortable and at home in her presence. It was a good start.

They walked to the theater and the movie was "Sergeant York." The tickets purchased, he bought popcorn and cokes for each of them. Fortunately he had worked all summer at American Furniture Factory and saved his money. T.J. admired the bravery and marksmanship that Gary Cooper's character portrayed. Jane enjoyed the movie but the newsreels of the war zone were graphic and full of horror. The coming attractions advertised "How Green Was My Valley" and Jane raved about wanting to see it. T.J. smiled and asked her if she would go with him to see it. Next, Jane invited him to her birthday party and he said, "Yes." By the end of the evening they were practically going steady.

That night was their first date so she didn't invite him in to listen to her record player in the living room. She thanked him for a lovely evening and said good night. No kiss on the first date. Maybe after her birthday party, they could kiss. These were new exciting feelings for both of them.

T.J. had a long walk home. Sections of town had a criminal element. In the future, T.J. never complained that as Jane took a few steps to a warm bed, he walked home in the rain, snow, or freezing wind. One night, he was approached by a lady offering herself if he would get a room. He ran. There was a camp of hobos by the train tracks. He often ran much of the way and it helped build muscles used for the "track" team. When he got home, he had no space of his own. He had to sleep in the bed with two younger brothers.

Tonight, he actually found himself smiling and giving a little skip now and then. He had never had a date and he felt it went really well. To him, she was the prettiest girl in high school and so easy to be with. He always had kept things to himself but he could talk to her. He was happy!

Sunday afternoon after church, Jane and Wilma, Doris and Dora were making fudge at Wilma's house. Jane glanced out of the window and then she saw T.J. walking by her house. She didn't mention it to the girls but she wondered what it meant. She was in unfamiliar territory and having feelings she had never felt before.

CHAPTER 3

WAR AT HOME

There were 100 million people involved in World War II (1939 -1945) from over 30 countries.

The war news alerted that the Japanese had taken over the Philippines and Singapore. Battle of Bataan and the Bataan Death March, (March and April of 1942), occurred when up to 650 Americans prisoners and thousands of Filipinos marched 60 miles without food or water, often ill or dying.

Good news came on June of 1942; Admiral Nimitz was credited with breaking the Japanese code and the loss to the Japanese Navy was so great that their naval power never recovered. This was only 7 months after Pearl Harbor and their sneak attack that obliterated much of our navy. Our industrial power was amazing!

Turnersville had lost several young men. Windows that displaced blue crosses were changed to gold crosses. People were sad as they passed by these homes but proud of the hometown men who served and they were grateful that their country was safe.

The war pain burst through the front door at the Carter home. Lily Adams was screaming, "They killed Tommy!"

Jane and her mother came running to their friend. Tommy Adams had grown up next door to Jane and when he turned 18, he was drafted into the infantry. The front page of the paper had carried the news about horrendous casualties and now Tommy was one of the causalities. Jane and the women stood holding each other. Eventually, they sat on the couch and tried to absorb the news. Jane brought a glass of water to Lily who was having trouble breathing. Jane was learning that the passing of a loved one brings pain like no other.

"God is here, Lily, to bring us comfort in our darkest moments," said Mary Carter and then she started to pray. "Dear God, you promised us a Comforter and we need the Comforter right now. Please be with Lily, Jane and me and all those touched by Tommy's passing into your hands." Jane saw Lily start to breathe deeply and sigh. That night Tommy's family would break bread with the Carters and the bond between them remained as long as the two mothers lived. They both loved Tommy and hated the war. In a short time, Jane had seen death twice and was beginning to wonder more deeply about life.

In church, Jane had been taught to "Believe and Obey." When she was in third grade, the choir had sung "Just as I Am" as Miss Leaner played the organ. Jane walked to the front of the church and asked to be saved. Evelyn joined her. They both wore pretty white organdy dresses to church three Sundays later, for their baptism. Jane's mother, sister and grandmother attended the eleven o'clock service to see her dipped into the baptismal water. Evelyn and her mother remained in the church office while Evelyn cried and refused to join her. She was afraid.

Later, Jane explained to Evelyn that, "You hold your nose so you don't drown. Nothing to it," she said. Mary Carter hoped indeed, that she didn't mean what she said about "nothing to it" and Jane received a mini sermon from her mother. She had given her life to Christ and now she must find His will for her life.

"There are two rules you are to obey," said her mother. "One rule is to love the Lord with all your might and the second is to love your neighbor as yourself. Then you try to find your purpose for being planted on God's earth. That's why you don't say it is nothing to it. By baptism, you have made a commitment."

The year was 1942, Jane would turn sixteen and she decided it was time to figure out how she could best serve. No one wanted to teach the twelve years old boys' class in Sunday School so she volunteered. She decided she would start the class with the Sports Section of the Sunday paper. This was particularly helpful if there were any articles praising the athletes. The boys all went to the high school football games. Jane was already plotting to convince T.J. to come and talk to her class. Everyone knew he was the hero on the football team.

The church had a list of elderly shut-ins. Jane's friend, Jean, planned to be a nurse and so Jane and Jean decided to visit a lady on the list. They walked to a very sad part of town.

The girls weren't sure that they had found the right house since there were no markers on the house. They knocked and a young woman answered the door. She was holding a baby. Two toddlers clung to her stained cotton smock. She acknowledged that the woman lived there but that she was bedridden. Excuses were offered rapidly as to why they couldn't see her. The girls were on a mission and they would not be deterred. It was a good thing too because the lady was in a desperate situation. The stench of urine was suffocating. Jean asked for a basin of water and soap. She traded the cookies they had brought for the things she needed. Meanwhile, Jane read the Bible and sang to the lady.

As soon as they left, Jane went straight home to get some nourishing soft food for the frail, elderly woman. She added extra bananas and biscuits with jam for the children.

Mary Carter was enlisted for getting a good doctor who would be willing to make an unpaid house call. There were few social services in 1940s.

Little security for health care was available if a person were elderly or poor. The government had put a cap on wage increases because of the war and scarce labor pool available. Incentives were allowed and thus a health insurance incentive furnished by the employer became very desirable. The Unions agreed to sanction these.

Mostly, people paid "fee for services." Often the most respected man in the community was the family doctor who would make house calls and accept a payment as much as the patient could pay. Hopefully, people went into medicine to take care of the patient, not just to make money. Health insurance wasn't a popular concept yet. The idea of suing your doctor was not usually an acceptable idea.

The patient and the doctor shared trust. The doctors didn't need high cost insurance coverage for suing a doctor was unheard of. People usually loved and respected their doctors and were realistic about the outcome. Often patients had life insurance but few had health insurance.

The typical family paid $148 a year for medical needs.

Some of the medical breakthroughs in the 40s were:

1st kidney dialysis machine

New medical technology based on radioactive products

Penicillin became a lifesaving antibiotic

Disposal diapers

Waksman discovered streptomycin

Blood Banks were established
Electronic Digital computer
The country had 6,572 hospitals by the end of the 40s.

CHAPTER 4
BIRTHDAY PARTY

Mary loved to entertain, but there had been precious little time or money for entertaining. Jane's father had lost his job as manager of a large retail store and compensated by becoming an alcoholic. He ruined his health and could not work. Mary had studied nutrition in college and due to people skills and accepting low pay, she became the hospital dietician. She was determined to decorate the house and give Jane her first birthday party, ever.

A huge pumpkin that Rob Carter, Jane's father, had brought down from the mountains already sat on the front section of the wraparound porch. It was a present from a friend who made cider from the apples he grew on his farm.

"Be sure it isn't hard cider and put some apples in a poke for fried apples pies," Mary laughed as she teased. She knew his friend had a still on the property. That was how mountain folk paid their doctor bills and bought shoes for their kids.

Reams of orange and black paper were purchased at Rose's five and Dime. Bats and pumpkins were fashioned to be place mats for the plentiful supply of treats. Crepe paper was strung through the house and colorful Halloween lanterns swung from the orange and black paper rope. Small pumpkins kin to the one on the porch made appearances in strange places. The house achieved a spooky look as a witch on a broomstick swung ready to hit you in the face if you didn't duck when you went into the dining room for refreshments. Carrie made Jane's favorite orange carrot cake. Emma creamed orange and black mints. Mugs filled with hot apple cider plus a bucket filled with ice and bottles of Orange Crush furnished the drinks. There was plenty for everyone.

Jane's party would be the topic of conversation the next week at school. The guests enjoyed the food, the decorations, the loud music, the Congo line through the halls and living room. Most discussed was what happened when someone turned off the lights. Mrs. Carter had rushed into the living room and turned them on again. There, sitting on T.J.'s lap, was Dora kissing him a big sloppy kiss on the mouth. Jane gasped, T.J. had the expression of a deer in the headlights and Dora just giggled.

"Keep the lights on!" Mrs. Carter was not happy.

Couples began to dance to favorite records they had brought to share. Bing Crosby and Frank Sinatra were favorites while the orchestras of Benny Goodwin, Guy Lombardo, Les Brown and Tommy Dorsey filled the house. T.J. asked Jane to dance. He hadn't really asked a girl to dance before and he wasn't sure if he could dance. He knew he had to try and fix this mess that Dora had caused.

"She jumped into my lap. I was surprised. Then she kissed me, Jane." T.J. was moving to the music but his mind was on the errand at hand. He had to clear himself with this girl that he couldn't stop thinking about. He had not recovered since that Saturday night when he first touched her hand. It was a strange obsession. He didn't understand the feelings.

Jane said, "Let's go into the hall and I'll teach you how to dance." They both laughed. A pattern was set as Jane helped T.J. maneuver the ways of teenage dating. No one in his family had ever been to high school, sent flowers for a prom, or apologized to a girl's mother.

He immediately found Mrs. Carter and said, "I am sorry." He didn't say that it would never happen with Jane for he was already plotting to try for a kiss that night.

Six boxes of Whitman's candy and a half a dozen silver charms for her bracelet were on her "present table." Her sister gave her the book, "Shakespeare, Simplified" and money arrived from her grandmother and Auntie. Her parents said the party was her present and she kissed them both in appreciation. Emma and Carrie took home many decorations and any leftover refreshments. Later Jane gifted each one with a box of candy. Now that she had a boyfriend, maybe she had better watch her weight, Jane thought.

T.J. gave her a silver compact from the jewelry store and had her name engraved on it. She cherished it the rest of her life.

It was late when everyone left but T.J. lingered and sat with Jane in the living room. Jane wanted to hear a boy's viewpoint of how things went. She was disappointed for T.J. never gossiped and felt most things were not any of his business. He was totally mellow. She and her friends talked about everything. T.J. kept things to himself.

As Jane chatted, T.J. moved closer to her and slowly put his arm on the back of the couch. That was uncomfortable so he moved closer and pulled her to him. She didn't resist. Then he kissed her, with passion new to both of them. They clung to each other and kissed again, this time longer and with no hesitancy. Jane said, "You better go."

T.J. was in love. On the long walk home, he didn't notice the October night's chill. A feeling of happiness kept him warm. He dreaded going home. It was hard to sleep with two younger brothers. Younger sisters squabbled a lot. He didn't blame his father for stopping at the filling station and having a "Jar" before coming home on some Saturday nights. The poor man worked hard at the furniture factory and all the money went to feed and clothe his family of seven. T.J. was at home as little as possible. His grades suffered because there was no quiet place to study. He flunked some classes his freshman year. He wanted to stay in school now because of her and he loved football too. Also, his good mother wanted him to "make something of himself."

Jane slipped into bed without brushing her teeth. It was very late and she heard her mother's steps in the hall.

"Jane are you still up?"

"Mother, what do you want?" Jane sounded as if she had been awakened from a deep sleep. She was very clever at mimicking voices.

"Nothing, dear. Sorry to wake you," her mother shuffled off to bed. Though she sounded sleepy, Jane could not go to sleep. It was her first kiss except when she had been at a party in Danville, Virginia and they played post office. She was visiting her cousin and the new girl in the group so she got several "letters." She couldn't say much for the kisses. Tonight made her toes curl. And she was really angry with Dora. She felt a jealousy that was new to her usual agreeable nature. As dawn approached, she fell asleep while planning her wedding.

CHAPTER 5

TO LOVE AGAIN

"Jane, get up. It's seven-thirty." Her dad reminded her of Sunday School and the Baptist Church.

"I don't feel well. Can I sleep just this once? I am still celebrating my birthday."

"No!" The response was quick and even though her dad didn't attend church, he had been sent on a mission by his wife. Not often did he get to enforce rules in his home and he relished doing it. Jane did want to see her friends and she also had taken on her new role as teacher for the boy's class.

Breakfast smelled good. The apples her dad had brought down from the hills were now fried in butter with a sprinkling of sugar. Fresh pork sausage from the same apple farm, grits and gravy plus hot buttered biscuits and molasses were on the table. This was a typical Sunday breakfast. Carrie and Emma liked to dress up and wear their church hats to the services on Sunday mornings. Her mom would do the cooking and her dad helped.

Jane wore a brown woolen skirt and jacket with an orange sweater that had been a gift from "the girls upstairs." She wore a tam for her hat. Because of the war and rationing, her new pink panties, a gift from her aunt, had buttons instead of the usual elastic. Jane also carried her lesson book, her Bible, and the Sports page from the Sunday paper. The first challenge of the day was to get the Sports page from her dad who was secretly proud of her mission.

The classroom was noisy and in confusion as the boys were "pretend fighting." As Jane walked in smiling and looking quite pretty. They got to their seats.

The attendance was taken. A check was marked by the student's name if he had brought his Bible and a coin for the collection basket. Baptist churches taught Bible study and tithing as important lessons for their youth.

"How many of you attended the game yesterday?" Jane asked. All hands went up except for one boy sitting in the back of the room. Play by play arguing was allowed for a while and that led into a discussion about rules and obeying," Jane asked.

"What is our rule book for life?"

The fellow in the back of the room raised his hand. Jane called on him.

"The Bible," he said. Jane smiled as she agreed with him.

"Love the Lord with all your might and love your neighbor as yourself, is the main rule," he said.

"Good for you!" Jane grinned this time and said, "That's the Golden Rule. Now everyone look up Matthew 7:12."

Sam was a big, loud voiced boy and could have been the bully of the class. He was the first to find the passage.

"Do to others as you would have them do to you. Matthew 7:12" Sam had a big smile denoting he was very pleased with himself.

"What does that mean, Sam?"

"If you have a bar of candy, you give a bite to your friend." Sam looked quite pleased with his answer.

"You give him half," came from the back of the room.

"That's too much. He wouldn't give me half," Sam whined. This time no self-satisfied grin.

Jane said, "Christ set the example of love and generosity. He would have given His friend the whole bar of candy. He gave much more for us. We should invite Christ into our lives and try to live as He did." Prayers were said and it was now time for Big Church. Many of the boys left for home. They seemed to like their new teacher.

Jane, much a teenager, went to sit in the balcony with her friends.

After church, Jane rushed home to tell her mother what a shocking thing that she and Peggy had witnessed at church.

"Old Mister Ward was holding hands with Polly, Mother. They were sitting in church and I saw them from the balcony." Jane sounded disgusted. "Mrs. Ward has only been dead about six months, Good Grief!"

"They have known each other for half a century, Jane," Mary Carter said defensively. "They are both good people who are lonely. I hope they fall in love and have some happiness."

"He loved his wife so much." Jane had seen them holding hands in church also and always thought it was so sweet.

"Just because you loved your wife and she died, it doesn't take anything away from loving again. Good marriages are a better risk to marry again than ones that had not been happy. God had generously opened Tom Ward's heart for more happiness. One love does not diminish the other. Polly loved "the doctor "and she deserves a chance to love again. She needs more to do than read books." Mary wanted to add, but didn't, and give advice.

"What about when they go to heaven, who will they be with?"

"There is no marrying in heaven. We shall all love each other in a way that humans don't and can't understand. We read of agape love but we are not capable of living it on earth."

That evening, T.J. was walking with Jane home from church. He was getting to hear all about Mr. Ward and Polly but he didn't seem as interested as Jane had anticipated he would be.

"Don't be the 'grief police,' Jane, it is kind of their business. If it makes them happy, who does it hurt?"

"It is not respectful to old Mrs. Ward."

"She's not here, now."

"Oh, T.J., everything is not always about being happy."

"Jane, it will work itself out."

"T.J., we have to hurry home," Jane was in a panic. "Turn around and close your eyes."

T.J. did as he was told but had no idea why.

Jane stepped out of her new pink panties and put them in her pocket. The button had come unbuttoned. No explanation was given.

T.J. stifled a laugh but he was too much of a gentleman to mention it, until 70 years later.

CHAPTER 6

HOMEFRONT

"Mr. Smith Goes to Washington" starring Jimmy Stewart appealed to the audiences of the early forties. It was Idealistic, hopeful and sincere while outsmarting some folks (or fools) in Washington. Jane and T.J. were at that movie for the Saturday night date. The faire of buttered popcorn and cokes was devoured while they watched a Mickey Mouse cartoon, coming attractions and then a news reel showing Allied Forces landing in North Africa. Annie's boyfriend was in that Division. He had gone into the Infantry as a Second Lieutenant and with battlefield promotions, he was now a Captain. He had written Annie that his aide had lost his life by jumping on a grenade that was thrown right in his path. Very sad but Biblical to give up your life for a friend. The war stories were filled with heroic acts performed for their fellow soldiers.

"One good thing about this war is that we are all in it together," said Mary Carter. She and Lily were having their evening chat on the front porch. "Jane's teacher is working on the rationing committee. I took her supper this afternoon and she was handing out the coupons for sugar. I hear the 'bootleggers' are now even using molasses to make 'white lightning.' I have a recipe for apple sauce instead of sugar for making my cakes."

"It would have to be mighty sweet apples," said Lily. She had spent the day rolling bandages for the Red Cross to use for the soldiers overseas. "I hear that Janet Lee has joined the WACS. "

Mary laughed, "Wouldn't you love to join the WACS ? Oh, but I hope Annie doesn't quit college and join up. Her classmates who didn't go to college are working at Du Pont. They are called the 'Rosie the Riveters.' I had to talk like a 'Dutch Uncle' to keep her headed to Farmville College. I went to college there and it has saved our family since Rob can't work."

"Women are having more opportunities than ever before because of the war. They are being praised for taking the jobs and getting good pay. It is now patriotic to work. The men are gone and someone is needed to build the tanks and in our town, the uniforms and parachutes. It is a great opportunity for those girls who live at your house. They leave the mountains and now have a real chance to improve their lives," Lily was animated as she talked. Mary was glad to see that she was slowly coming out of the deep grief she had felt when her son had been killed in the war.

Both women had been opposed to getting into a war at all but now everyone was on the same team and the country was united. Adults bought War Bonds. The schools sold 10 cent stamps and Jane had filled one stamp book already. She and T.J. collected scrap metal for the scrap drives. Movie stars were entertaining the troops and some famous stars like Jimmy Stewart had volunteered to serve. John Wayne helped with patriotic movies; he performed in fourteen movies. Bob Hope delighted the troops all over the world. The young single girls entertained at USO dances. Women of all ages gave out refreshments at train stations or anyplace that service men might assemble away from the base. Families tried to keep spirits up and mail became the lifeline for this. Letters flew back and forth to help solidify relationships and help keep soldiers from being lonely. There were letters censored. A new item used was very thin air mail paper.

Patriotic duty was real for all walks of life; democracy in action. Everyone was in the same class concerning service in the war since anyone's family member could have been drafted into service. All knew of button panties instead of elastic, no gas for non-essentials and even ladies' stockings were scarce.

T.J. and Jane walked home from the movie, hand and hand. They, neither one, could think of a better place to be or a better person to be with. They were experiencing "first love." The feeling that you were "at home" with this person. You could share your deepest feelings and be safe in doing so. Jane was busy talking about the movie and T.J. stopped her and turned her toward him and said, "I love you, Jane Carter."

Jane caught her breath and quietly said, "I love you T.J. Jennings."

They had never declared their love in so many words. Somehow, it made a difference. They were a couple. It didn't change the physical part as T.J. knew the rules that said kissing and holding each other were enough. They didn't realize until many years later that this relationship was what set him on the path for a happy, good life and would make her feel loveable and able to express love.

CHAPTER 7

COME SIT A SPELL

The large wraparound porch had rocking chairs, a swing, Adirondack chairs and a feeling of "Welcome, come sit a spell." Mary Carter and her husband sat there on most summer evenings. No one whom they knew had air conditioning except Polly, and that was only in one room. The days were very hot and humid but the evenings cooled off. Anyone coming down their street would say "hello" and wave, and if they wanted to discuss the war or conditions of the day, they would stop to chat. One visitor who came most summer evenings was Miss Annie. She lived alone and though she owned an apartment house and two duplexes, she didn't know many people to talk to. Jane would exit when she saw her coming, for Miss Annie was the most boring person Jane had ever met.

That night Miss Annie was concerned about rationing. "The Daily Bulletin announced that now they are rationing shoes." Miss Annie hadn't bought shoes in twenty years and had no notion of buying them any time soon but she could feel sorry for anyone who needed new shoes. "That's added to shortages of rayon, wool, leather, rubber and even metal for buckles. Then we have no gas, no sugar. I don't drive a car and I don't bake. I do like sugar in my morning tea. I wish that Mr. Hitler would, 'God forgive me'," and she crossed herself, and didn't finish what Hitler might do so she wouldn't be so inconvenienced.

Rob Jennings was reading the newspaper when Miss Annie had arrived. He picked it up and started reading aloud after hearing Miss Annie's unwelcomed comments on the war. "See here, where they are starting to do hydraulic fracturing in West Virginia. That will produce more coal." Neither woman knew what hydraulic fracturing was.

"Did you ladies know that the U.S. has taken the fashion world away from France since France had surrendered to the Germans? Teachers' salaries have gone up to $1,441." Rob was glad he could interrupt the negative conversation that Miss Annie always wanted to share. "Those Tupperware parties are popular. You been to one, Miss Annie?"

"No, I don't believe in trying to get your guests to buy stuff. It doesn't seem Southern." Miss Annie was leaving, "Bye, now."

"You come back, you hear." Mary said as she looked at her husband. "You drove her away again. I feel sorry for the poor soul. All she has is money and that doesn't make you happy."

It would help, Roy thought, but he didn't say anything since he couldn't seem to shake his alcoholic problem. He was anxious and deeply depressed much of the time. Whiskey was the only thing that helped. He was upset that Jane kept pouring out any bottles of whiskey that she found.

Polly stopped by on her way home from the market. She had been reading "Fountainhead" by Ann Rand. She wanted Mary to read it. "It isn't for Jane to read. I have another new book for her, "A Tree Grows in Brooklyn," by Betty Smith. Rob, you would like "For Whom the Bell Tolls" by Ernest Hemingway. Reading gets my mind off the war except the book by Hemingway but it is a different war, anyway." Polly was Mary's most intellectual friend. She had been married to the doctor who founded their local hospital but he was dead now and Polly had retired from her job as nursing supervisor at the hospital.

"When will I get the time?" Mary had a house filled with "guests" and worked as head dietician at the only hospital in the county. She had a husband who was an alcoholic and two daughters in their teens.

"I just saw Miss Annie leave. You could read instead of listening to her complain." Polly was outspoken and knew Mary was too kind for her own health. She had some heart problems and COPD plus high blood pressure. Polly had been her nurse when Mary had to be admitted to the hospital a few years back. "Now get by yourself and read. Nurse's orders. Don't feel guilty if you take some time for yourself. I'll bring down 'Fountainhead' when I'm finished."

Jane came rushing out and was very excited, "Miss Paige Ann just died." Six weeks before, Miss Paige Ann's handyman, Amos, had heard her scream and found her on the floor in the living room. Amos reported she that had a bad fall. He had taken her to rest at a cousin's "care home."

Miss Paige Ann had been president of the Republican Women's Auxiliary. She dressed in the latest fashions, always had her hair and nails done at the local beauty parlor where she learned and enjoyed the latest gossip. She was critical of other people who were less properly attired and informed.

Mary Carter had never been allowed into Paige Ann's house though Paige Ann was a frequent visitor at the Carter's house, particularly at supper time. Several times, Mary had given Paige Ann a ride to church functions but she was never invited into the house. Even when it was snowing or raining, Paige Ann was on the porch waiting for a ride but no one had been into the house since her parents had died. Polly, jokingly, said that maybe she had them mummified.

Amos reported that Paige Ann hadn't wanted any visitors except for him since she said that she trusted Amos to take care of her house. None of her friends knew where she was. When they tried to find her, there was a restraining order sworn out by a lawyer whose office was in another city. Paige Anne's previous lawyer had been fired. Amos was now her Conservator. Paige Anne was now dead at 76 years old.

The mystery of Paige Ann's death was the topic of conversation everywhere. Jane really wanted to walk by Paige Ann's house and see if that Amos fella was living there. After church, she and T.J. took a detour.

"Let's go and look through the window." Jane, curious as usual, was determined to see inside this mystery house.

"Aw, Jane. I think that is trespassing." T.J. wasn't as curious, by nature, as Jane was. He had to weigh getting into trouble with the law or with Jane and he knew who would win out.

"Come on, we can go around the back and if anyone says anything we can say we are looking for a dog. It isn't a lie if we don't say it is our dog. I would like to have a dog, wouldn't you?"

"Your mom won't let you have a dog, Jane."

Jane was already standing tippy toe, looking into a window.

"The bed is stacked high with stuff. The walls are lined with plastic covering everything. You couldn't walk in there unless you were real skinny and went sideways." Jane was ready to try a sneak into another room. She went around to the front porch where she could see into the living room. There was a grand piano, next to a harp and a spinning wheel. The plastic covered boxes lined the walls just as in the bedroom.

Suddenly, the big wooden door flung open and she was staring down the barrel of a shot gun. "She's looking for a dog!" T.J. said, as he grabbed her by the arm and they took the steps two by two and ran for a block before they stopped and started laughing.

"You are going to get us killed," T.J. said as he hugged her. Jane pulled away because they were in public.

Jane went home and told her mother all she had seen through the windows in Paige Ann's house. She told her about the man with the shot gun and how T.J. was fast in his thinking to tell the man that they were looking for a dog.

"We didn't stop to find out whether or not he had seen our imaginary dog."

Mary Carter didn't laugh. "Stay away from that house, Jane," she said emphatically.

"Why were all of those things, there?" Jane was using her hands to show how piled up everything was.

"Jane, you are too inquisitive! It's going to get you into real trouble someday. I'm surprised T.J. didn't stop you."

Mary continued, "Paige Anne was a hoarder. It is a sickness of values. I remember once you valued getting what you wanted over obeying me." When Jane was starting seventh grade, Mary had decided to let her buy her outfit for the first day in Junior High. She dropped Jane and a friend off at Marshall's. Mary had tied the money in a handkerchief and pinned it to the inside of Jane's jacket.

When she picked Jane and her friend up, Jane had a parakeet, cage and feed. No new clothes. She was allowed to keep the bird but she had to wear her old clothes until she got a new sweater and saddle oxfords for her Christmas present. She was old enough now to learn the good and bad about money.

Mary wasn't finished with explaining, "Paige Ann may have thought that money or things would make her happy and secure. People find that the more they have, the more they want. There is never enough. Along with this, is the fear that someone will take their stuff."

Mary continued, "God has definite instructions about money and possessions. It is mentioned all through the Bible. Look in

Proverbs and in the New Testament. Get your Bible and mine, please. One that addresses a need that Paige Ann had is in Matthew 6: 19 'Do not lay up for yourselves treasurers on earth, where moth and rust destroy and where thieves break in and steal. But lay up for yourselves treasures in heaven…where your treasure is, there your heart will be also."

"Ecclesiastes 5:10, 'He who loves money will not be satisfied with money' …..and Ecclesiastes goes on to say that the more we have, the more we spend and none of this brings lasting happiness. Paige Ann loved her possessions more than she loved anything or anyone else. Since God created everything, everything is His. We are blessed to use it while we are here."

"Jane, you read Exodus 23:2"

Jane read the passage.

"Now what does it tell you?"

"You are not to follow the crowd. Just because Peggy has a parakeet, doesn't mean I should covet one." Jane giggled.

"Now Jane, I am serious. God's word tells us all about money and how it is to be used. We are not to be lazy but work and pay for what we need. We are to help those in need. That includes not buying things you don't need just because they are on sale, a problem you have, Jane."

Mary wanted to be sure that Jane understood that money was very important but for the right reasons. She wanted Jane to know that greed and pride can come with wealth because the person might feel that it was all because they did it themselves and leave God out of it.

"You are not what you own, Jane. You use God's gifts but they are God's gifts while you are here for the life span He has given you."

Jane was beginning to fidget. "It is like the sex lecture. You are telling me more than what I want to know,"

"One last thing. Proverbs 1:8 instructs you to listen to your parents. Remember, Jane, I want you to be able to care of me someday," As usual Mary ended her conversation on a light note and laughed.

CHAPTER 8

HANDS ACROSS THE OCEAN

"Jane hurry, the president is on."

President Roosevelt's "Fireside Chats" were cherished by the Carter family. They didn't just like the President, they loved him. He was talking about the cherished relationship between United States and Great Britain. Tonight, President Roosevelt even mentioned that a British ship would be docked at Norfolk, Virginia for the Christmas season.

"We need to show hospitality to our fellow Brits. Families in Ireland, Scotland and England have all shared their homes with our soldiers," President Roosevelt proclaimed.

"They have so little to share since the Germans have bombed continually but they share," said Mary Carter.

Jane guessed that her mother was thinking of another patriotic project. Mary sent meals to the team of volunteers who were working on the vouchers for rationing. A map on the Carter's wall traced battles and the location of troops. The family was involved in selling and buying War Bonds and Victory stamps at the schools and the theater. Jane bought the ten cent victory stamps and had filled one book already. Her dad found an old abandoned car from a farm to add to Jane's scrap drive collection. The Carter family, like most of the whole country, was patriotic.

With several phone calls to the Red Cross, Mary Carter and her friend, Polly Stone, completed plans for two British sailors to spend Christmas in Turnersville. One Limey homebased in London and the other fellow was from Scotland. They were to sleep at Polly's house and eat meals with the Carters. Jane and her older sister, Annie, would play hostess. T.J. liked his job as male companion to the group who were welcomed as honored guests. There was Christmas caroling along with Christmas pageants, Wassail Bowl and egg nog parties plus many dinner invitations. This War Effort made the War seem very distant as they sat by the fireplace and sang the hit tunes of the day......"Don't Sit Under the Apple Tree With Anyone Else But Me," "White Christmas" and many other songs that people on both sides of the ocean enjoyed.

Jane called the English sailor "Bub" but when the family got a thank you note, it was signed Bob. Slight accent incident!

Teens are self-centered and this trait inoculated the teenagers of the early forties from missing any fun. Many younger boys did try to join the Armed Forces but mostly parents intervened in time to grab them back into high school. There were no "foreigners" living in Turnersville and most families had been there for several generations. One family had moved thirty miles in a hundred years when they came down out of the Blue Ridge Mountains. Their relatives remained up there with their whiskey stills.

Turnersville had segregated schools. This seemed very natural since it was all anyone had experienced. Mrs. Roosevelt had pushed for better segregated schools in the South and as far as the kids were concerned they didn't think about the right or wrong of it. Except one day, Jane asked her minister if they could invite some of the black students to the Baptist Church to discuss "things." There was resounding "No." "They were to stay with their own kind" permeated in the South. "You know who that is" was a phrase that Jane hated.

In school, Jane went out of her way to be inclusive of everybody. Out in the adult world, there was the Colored (black) Section, the Cotton Mill Section and the rest were white collar workers topped by the elite who owned the factories. The husband represented the family so it was helpful if he had a white collar job or preferably i he owned something besides a truck, a gun and a dog.

The radio and the newspaper furnished the family's war news. Jane would dial the radio to her favorite music station until news time. Then everyone in the family would sit and listen.

Roosevelt asks for 53 billion dollars for the war. (488 ships were built that year, 1943). U. S was sending 100, 000 Japanese to camps. Draft age was now 18. Gas rationing was being enforced and people had to apply and justify the gallons they could buy at fifteen cents a gallon.

War news that year featured the Allied Forces landing in North Africa. The British were flying bombers over Germany and made heavy hits on some German cities. U.S B-17's bombed Rouen in France. Naples, Italy was hit by B-24's. Bad news on the radio blasted that Japanese forces had moved into the Philippines, Manila and Singapore. Major General Doolittle led a group bombing over Tokyo. Jane listened but had no concept of the lives ending and the horror that the bombs were causing. She was sixteen and gas rationing was serious business. No trips in the car unless "necessary" and it was hard for teens to justify what they consider necessary. T.J.'s family didn't have a car so Jane and T.J. were joined by more friends in doing a lot of healthy walking.

T.J. and Jane had been dating for about a year. T.J. was the star of the football team and Jane was his biggest fan. He loved having someone at the game rooting especially for him. She was proud of him and he was proud of her. They complimented each other. She wrote for the school paper, sang with the Glee Club and acted in every play the school or church performed. She was often enthused and he was mellow. She knew the social rules and he was comfortable in learning them. She made decisions and he liked to please her so he agreed. It bothered her that he didn't plan much. They had the ability to converse easily, enjoy and work toward the same things. They felt understood and appreciated. Each brought out the best in the other; the sides of themselves that they liked. They trusted each other. Both teenagers had outside jobs and both also were called on for emotional support for their families. They took care of things. They were good kids.

Asked by his fellow football friends if they had "done it" and T.J. said, "We are happy with what we have." There was no doubt that they were attracted to each other but some of their classmates had gotten pregnant and left school to work in the factories. Neither one wanted that. Jane had her Baptist fear of disgracing her mother and disobeying the Bible. Reputations were valued above gold for men and women. Girls were appreciated as ladies of strong character. Men were expected to be polite and honor women as wives and mothers. Rapes among high school and college students were rare.

T.J. agreed to come to one of her Sunday School classes. Having committed his life to Christ as age 12, the age of the boys in her class, he was the perfect one to talk to them. The fact that now he was Captain of the football team, added enthusiasm for attendance.

T. J. had never attended church without wearing a coat and tie. That Sunday, he looked handsome in a blue sports coat, white shirt and blue tie. Jane proudly introduced him as T.J. Jennings, Captain of the Bull Dogs.

T.J. carried a football. He said, "I'm going to ask a question and if you know the answer, raise your hand, I'll pass the football to you. But first, Jane is going to read eight selections from Proverbs. (He didn't want to embarrass slower readers). Listen, the answers are hidden in the verses." T.J. said, "Proverbs was written by King Solomon, we are told that he was very wise. Here goes."

"Don't lose sight of good planning and insight. Hang on to them" Prov. 2:21

"People who accept correction are on the pathway to life. Those who ignore it will lead others astray."
Prov. 10:1

"To learn, you must love discipline; it is stupid to hate correction." Prov. 12:1

"It is possible to give freely and become wealthy' but those who are stingy will lose everything." Prov. 11:24

"The Lord hates those who don't keep their word, but He delights in those who do." Prov. 12:22

"A hothead starts a fight, a cool tempered person tries to stop it." Prov. 15:18

"Gentle words bring life and health; a deceitful tongue crushes the spirit." Prov. 15:3

"A foolish child brings grief to a father and bitterness to a mother." Prov. 17:25

T.J. thanked Jane, smiled and stood tall and confident before these young fellows who admired him on the football field and looked forward to him as a leader.

T.J. asked. "Should you plan your life or just do what is easy?" Hands went up and T.J. passed the football. It was caught and the answer was. "No sir, you will flunk out of school if you do what is easy and don't study."

"Good answer and in life there are no short cuts. For football games we practice and plan our game, even study the other team's tactics. Ball back please."

T.J. used football analogies, "The coach calls you out in front of the team. What do you do?"

Ball passed. Caught and the answer, "You take the correction and learn or you won't be part of the team."

T.J. said, "That goes for school, parents and anyone in authority. Don't listen to your friends. Be smart!"

T.J. asked "What about being greedy, not sharing and giving the other person a turn?"

The answer given was about not hogging the ball when you are in a football game.

T.J. explained, "God means this for all of life. The greatest gift given was when Christ gave His life as a sacrifice for all who believed in Him and accepted his sacrifice for their sins."

The ball passing and catching went smoothly with the lessons about obeying parents, avoiding fights, keeping their word. T.J. then said, "A boy does what he wants, but a man does what needs to be done. Be men!"

T.J. surprised Jane when he explained that, "Christians were to treat the body as their temple: eat right, exercise, not drink whiskey or smoke. Body, mind and spirit! This also helped in sports which prepares you for life. You learn that sometimes you lose, how to get along with your team, how to follow the rules and to accept authority because there is always someone higher up than you." He had taken his assignment seriously.

Jane thanked T.J. who said the prayer ending in "May the Love of God, the Grace of Christ and the Fellowship of the Holy Spirit be with everyone here and with their families and friends."

He turned to Jane, winked and said, "Let's go to church." They sat in the balcony and he held her hand.

CHAPTER 9

THE LORD'S WORK

After church, Jane wanted to talk about the sermon, "Dr. McCabe said that we all have a purpose in life. That is to serve the Lord but how do we know what our purpose is?"

T.J. said, "Jane, don't you want to be happy? That's what I want, to be happy. We have the war, our parents struggle and they don't seem to be all that happy. I want to be happy!"

"Happy is not a verb, you have to do something to make the world a better place." Jane was using her hands now to emphasize her words. T.J. would rather be holding hands than having this discussion which seemed remote when his concerns were football, having enough money to take Jane to the movie, and passing the algebra test on Monday.

Several weeks later, after seeing "Philadelphia Story" with Jimmy Stewart and Katherine Hepburn, they sat in the living room and talked about the movie.

T.J. said, "I have a problem. One of the fellows on the team asked me how he could be saved. I said go to church but I know that was not the right answer and I feel guilty that I didn't have a better answer."

"Yeah, there are 'church Christians' and there are 'Believers.'" Jane wanted to help T.J. but she had never told anyone how to be saved either. She sure did not want to miss this opportunity for both of them to have that experience. "First you say, we all have done wrong and we need forgiveness. So we admit our sins and ask for God to forgive them."

"I don't feel right asking him to tell me his sins, Jane." T.J. was sure he didn't want to do this.

"He just has to tell God. Then ask forgiveness and for Christ to come into his life as his sacrifice and friend. Then going to church will help him learn Christ's teachings. Be sure to thank God for saving him and for the promise of life everlasting. Tell him we will pray for him."

T.J. said, "Jane I'll bring him over to your house and you can do it."

"Well, we can do it together," said Jane. "Better do it quickly before we lose him." The next Sunday, T.J. took Jeff to his church and that afternoon they came to Jane's house for the homemade peach ice cream and sugar cookies. They sat in the living room around the coffee table.

Jane began, "T.J. said you were interested in learning more about faith. We believe in God, Christ and the Holy Spirit. They are one, just like T.J. is a son, a football player and a friend, all are part of who he is. All three were there when the earth and the first people, Adam and Eve, were created. The first people, like us to-day, disobeyed God. They wanted to do things their way, just as we want to do things our way. They weren't grateful to God nor were they obedient."

T.J. was getting a little anxious about how long it was taking. He thought they were just going to tell him about 'being saved.' "Jane, maybe we could have the shorter version."

Jane said "All right, we must invite Christ into our lives as Lord and Savior. He will change us from inside, out. Man was so sinful

41

that a sacrifice had to be made. Christ as part of the Godhead came to live on earth and to die as that sacrifice. When you believe, then you are promised eternal life. Christ dies, rises and gives the Holy Spirit to enter your life as a counselor and comforter. You will want to follow Christ's teachings and that means attending church and studying the Bible and praying. T.J. do you want to say that part?" Jane had prepared a prayer for T.J. to read.

T.J. read, "God, I'm sorry for my sins. Right now I turn from my sins and ask you to forgive me. Thank you for sending Jesus Christ to die on the cross as my Savior. Jesus, I ask you to come into my life and be my Lord, Savior and the Holy Spirit to be my guide and friend. Thank you for forgiving me and giving me eternal life. I do believe. In Jesus name I pray, Amen."

There was silence and Jeff had tears in his eyes. He said, "I want what T.J. has and this seems the way for me to head in the right direction." Then he took the prayer and read it.

Jane said, "As you read the prayer and meant it, you can be sure that God has forgiven you and received you into His family."

Jane handed him a Bible that her church presents to new believers and gave him a big hug.

T.J. said, "Let's go. I'll see you tonight, Jane."

T.J. was glad he had a long walk home for it had been an emotional afternoon. Jeff lived near him. They said very little on their walk home.

CHAPTER 10

THE PROM

The Senior Prom was coming up. Peggy didn't have a date. Somehow, this had become T.J.'s problem.

"It is Peggy's senior year and you are president of the class and captain of the baseball team," Jane thought that should have its perks.

"Jane, I don't like to get dates for people. It never works out," T.J. had been in this situation before.

"Peggy's mom called and asked me to find someone to take Peggy to her last prom. She even said you could drive their car." T.J. had driven the football bus to take the class to Fairy Stone Park. Peggy's parents liked him and they had watched him play football with their son who had graduated two years before their daughter, Peggy.

"They have to rent a tuxedo and the football guys all have dates already." T.J. knew he would end up trying to find someone, since he never could turn Jane down. One idea was to get Ray, who was the Disc Jockey for the night, to bring her. He already had a tux but he wouldn't be able to dance with his date unless T.J. played a few of the records for him. T.J. didn't mind doing that part because he didn't know how to jitter-bug and he could play some of his and Jane's favorite records.

"Okay, I'll l try." He didn't want Jane's input until he asked Ray.

The news that night was bad. Two more local boys had died in battle. Jane knew both of them. She remembered that the one named George Washington was really tall for his desk. One day, he shared that he liked his margarine before they put coloring in it. Funny, the things you remember when someone dies. She had played with Billy, the other boy who died, when they were kids. Her mother had tutored Billy in seventh grade. They were studying "American History for Young Americans." The book said that Young Americans should see history as a whole, see events in relation to each other and how they will play a role someday in the story. This became Jane's favorite class, resulting in her lifelong love of history books that told a story, not just dates and dry facts.

There were no services for the young soldiers. They had fallen in France and would be buried there. They had come from poor circumstances, lied about their ages and gone to fight for freedom. It was a freedom they would never enjoy. Jane hoped that those who were safe at home would appreciate the sacrifices being made to keep them all safe. Again, she made a commitment to try and make the world a better place and that she had paid for her time on earth.

Jane lay in bed that night and thought about her old seventh grade history book and then went and retrieved it from the book case in the hall. That was the only text book that Jane had ever saved. It was full of stories instead of dates and battles fought. Maybe that would help her to fall asleep. She had found it tucked in next to the Compton's Encyclopedia that her mom was still paying installments on.

She read that North America was settled by Europeans, mostly from England and France. They brought their customs and language. It was a New Word and these settlers had new ideas. Jane flipped the pages to the Civil War and smiled as she read that the South was on the defensive as the North set out to conquer them. She read that Stonewall Jackson performed exploits in the Valley of Virginia which are among the most brilliant in military history. Jane giggled as she remembered having to remind her grandpa that "we lost the war." She thought of Billy, and how her mom had tutored her and Billy before an exam by calling out questions and patiently explaining the cause and effect of happenings that went on in history.

At school, T.J. cornered Ray after manual training class. They were making picture frames to be used by their families for the forthcoming senior class portraits. "I need a favor, Ray. I know you are going to spin the records for Prom. I figure that you haven't asked a girl for a date yet."

"No, don't plan to. I'll be busy," said Ray. He was taking his job very seriously.

T.J. began his campaign. "You know Peggy Mercer. She is really nice and she doesn't have a date."

"I don't have money for a corsage and we neither one have a car."

T.J. said, "I'll get the corsage if you'll go. I'll spin some records so you can take a break and have refreshments and I know you love to jitter bug. Come on, Ray."

Ray would love to be with T.J. He wasn't a football/baseball player like T.J. who was a super athlete and a really nice guy. He also would like to participate with the eats and dance. He knew if T.J. said he would do something, he would do it. He said, "Okay."

"Can we help you choose the records?" T.J. wanted to be sure that some of Jane's and his favorites would be played.

Ray agreed, "Yes, the radio station will let us borrow all we want if we get them back the next day." Ray was enjoying the idea now.

The morning before the prom, Peggy with Ray and Jane and T.J. went to choose the records that would furnish memories for kids who were going to the Junior-Senior Prom. Jane made the list of records that the boys would pick up the next day. The list:

"Swinging On A Star" Bing Crosby
"Chattanooga Choo Choo" Glenn Miller
"I'll Never Smile Again" Tommy Dorsey
"Green Eyes" Jimmy Dorsey
"Elmer's Tune" Glenn Miller
"Anniversary Song" Al Jolson
"I Love You For Sentimental Reasons" Nat King Cole
"Jingle Jangle Jingle" Kay Kyser
"I've Got A Girl From Kalamazoo" Glen Miller
"Taking A Chance on Love" Benny Goodman
"I'll Be With You In Apple Blossom Time" Jo Stafford
"I Don't Want To Set The World On Fire" Ink Spots
"Making Believe" Ella Fitzgerald and Ink Spots
"You Always Hurt The One You Love" Doris Day
"Till The End Of Time" Perry Como
"Paper Doll" Mills Brothers
"Blues In The Night" Woody Herman
"I'll Be Seeing You" and "Swinging On A Star" Bing Crosby

The radio manager (Ray's father) who had given his permission, shook his head and said, "Don't you have enough? We will have to celebrate Country Western Music for twenty four hours."

Ray said, "Dad, everyone has a favorite and there are so many good songs."

"Okay, five more and that is it. I'll have one of the guys bring them to the Country Club. They will bring them back after the Prom is over. Just call the station. Don't break any of them."

"We won't, I promise." Ray was feeling good about the whole project. The Country Club had a good record player and he could select several records to play consecutively.

"Don't Fence Me In," "White Cliffs of Dover," "Always" (for Jane), "I'll Walk Alone," and "White Christmas" even though it was the last of May, 1946, were the five they chose.

The purple orchid corsages were delivered to the girls. They were the perfect flowers for a Senior Prom. Gardenias were usually sent but a girl had bragging rights when she got an orchid. Ray's dad had heard about the deal and was glad his son had a friend like T.J. and that Ray was taking a date, also. He paid for the orchids and two white boutonnieres. Peggy's mom let T.J. drive their blue convertible. The girls would not allow them to put the top down on the way to the dance. The ride home, in the moon light, with the top down and a breeze that smelled sweet of magnolia would make driving with one hand necessary.

At the Prom, the music was romantic and lights were low. T.J. pulled Jane so close that it looked as if their bodies were one. Then he decided to surprise her with "the dip" that Ray had taught him. "Taking A Chance on Love" was playing and suddenly T.J. got frisky and started to show Jane what he had learned, that she hadn't taught him. It was such fun as he twirled her around and then ended with a dip as he almost dropped her. They both broke out in peals of laughter.

"The Peg and Ray date went well," Jane said as she thanked T.J. again for making her friend happy.

"You were the prettiest girl there, Jane."

"Oh, T.J. you are prejudice." Years later, she would wish she had accepted his compliments more graciously.

"I love you, Jane Carter." "I love you T.J. Jennings." That would become a secret between them. Any time they said the whole name, it was like saying "I love you." "Always" would be their song of love forever.

The dancing had ended, this was their last prom, ever!

CHAPTER 11

WAR TIME WEDDING

Glad to be home, the common denominator for most of the returning G I.s was that they wanted to get married. Since the U.S. hadn't been bombed like much of the rest of the world, the factories were furnishing much of the world's goods. The economy was booming. Joe had been dating Annie when he was a cadet at V. P.I. Annie loved going to the dances and began to love this sweet Southern gentleman. While he was "Over Seas," Joe had written beautiful love letters to Annie. He and his men had fought hard in the African campaign and now that the war was ending, he was coming home. He wanted to be with the beautiful blond he had dreamed about. He wanted to get married. He didn't want to wait!

Annie loved college and was more of a scholar than Jane. The dilemma was that though she loved Joe, she wanted to finish her education. They decided to get married and live in one of the trailers designated for married students. Using the G.I. Bill, Joe would get his master's degree and she would continue classes also but now at V.P.I.in Blacksburg, Virginia.

The wedding was to take place immediately at the First Baptist Church in Turnersville. The Carter family panicked. Jane, who had never even been to a wedding, was in charge. Her Uncle Bill, agreed to come from Richmond, walk with Annie down the aisle and give her away. Jane arranged for the minister and music at the church. Next, she needed to pick out china and silverware so they could be registered in the bride's and groom's names. She chose pottery with pretty pink flowers and silverware that looked very durable.

What to wear became a problem since Annie was in the middle of exams and had no time at all to give advice. Jane went to Leggett's Department Store and tried on a tomato red (looked like cream of tomato soup) crepe dress and said, "that will do." She wore it that one time, only. Crepe dresses were not her style.

The reception was the problem that Carrie, Emma and Polly solved. Polly had a crystal punch bowl and all the elegant service to go with it. Carrie made the tiered wedding cake. Ella hummed the wedding march as she fixed all of the condiments and she was included in preparing the ingredients for the dainty tea sandwiches.

T.J. managed to get a buddy to be an usher with him.

Joe picked Annie up at her college and they drove to Turnersville for the wedding. He and his best man, an Army buddy, were to bunk at Polly's.

Everyone was excited! Jane was babbling about the preparations when Annie showed her what she had bought to wear for the wedding. It was a two piece lime green spring suite.

"Oh, Annie, at the altar, we are going to look like one of Mama's dinner salads when she just serves lettuce and a slice of tomato." There was no time to exchange outfits since the wedding was to be the next day. They both laughed! Then they tried on their hats. Annie had a hint of a veil but neither hat saved the comic mixture of colors that the bride and maid of honor were to wear for the wedding the next day.

Joe, now a major, wore his uniform. T.J. and his buddy wore suites and ties. Annie wore a white orchid and Jane had a white gardenia corsage. The flowers in the church were from Polly's garden. Everyone wore a grin since both families were proud of the couple and approved of the marriage. Rob Carter was too anxious to attend the wedding but he approved of Joe and thought he was a good man. It was a typical wedding in war time, not a "fashion" but a "feeling" wedding. They lived in the moment.

The big house lent itself to a lovely wedding reception. The dining room had white linen table cloths on both tables. The punch bowl and cups glistened while ready to be filled with champagne punch. The wedding cake and dainty plates were arranged next to silver salad forks. White tulips were the flowers that decorated the room. Plates were filled with English tea sandwiches separated by colorful peeks of green parsley and purple pansies. Green and white handmade mints made Ella proud.

The wedding was a success. The couple took off in a Dodge convertible for the Greenbrier Hotel. At home, Jane and T.J. sat in the living room listening to their big band music. They neither one realized how important their relationship was. Jane was planning for college and to teach school, motivate kids and write books. She didn't anticipate being a famous author. She was a story teller and she wrote as she talked, nothing poetic or soul searching. She was curious and she loved her country and the stories that were lived out daily. T.J. had little to say except that he just wanted to be happy. He didn't plan anything, just let it happen. This bothered Jane who didn't want to have to push her husband and wished for someone who challenged her. She loved T.J. but she was young and didn't realize that what she really needed was his love and support in order to fulfill her dreams. He made her feel good about herself. T.J. loved Jane and wanted to make her happy so he just tried to do what she wanted, never guessing he was losing her because he didn't share his dreams of being a coach someday. He didn't even mention that he had been offered a scholarship but it wasn't enough to cover his needs. He said nothing to change the image of someone who was going to drift. There was no one to push and encourage him. Jane didn't want to play that role for she knew she could be a shrew and she didn't want that for either of them. The warmth of their kisses and passion of their love would have to wait for 70 years before they were examined in honesty.

The next day, Emma and Carrie wanted to talk about the wedding and the food. They were so proud of themselves. They were disappointed in the hats that the guests and Jane and Annie wore. "They weren't church hats! At our church, the ladies compete to see who can have the most beautiful hat. Some ladies have 20 or more hats," Emma said.

"I keep my favorite hat in a hat box with a handle," said Carrie. "It has green peacock feathers that seem to change colors as they frame the hat. Everyone wants to borrow it but I will never lend it for fear I won't get it back."

"I saved and got a one of a kind hat 'cause I don't want to see someone else wearing the same hat I had on," said Ella. Ella had about a dozen children and all of her girls wore tams or some kind of head covering for church on Sunday.

"You should come and see the ladies parade their hats up and down the aisles on Sunday. There are mink trims or silver fox flairs. My goodness, the flowers that decorate those hats are in all colors," said Carrie.

Jane shared, "I saw a hat I fell in love with in Holt's window but it is too expensive. I don't want to even ask Mama for it and my money from my job is laughable compared to Holt's prices. It is a full brimmed straw hat with flowers of every color you can think of. I have a Kelly-green suite for Easter and I would just love that hat." Carrie whispered Jane's wish to Mary Carter who stopped by Holt's and put the hat on lay-a-way to be picked up by Easter.

Easter Morning arrived and Jane went out on the porch to see if T.J. had sent her Easter corsage. There it was, a purple orchid.

Mary and Rob called her to come to their bed room. There was her most beautiful hat, not on the bed for that is bad luck, but on Rob's head. There was group hug, careful not to crush her hat.

Jane walked to church wearing her beautiful hat, her new Kelly green suit sporting its purple orchid. She wore brown alligator pumps and carried a handbag to match. She had never paid much attention to her looks but that Easter Sunday she felt beautiful.

CHAPTER 12
A PASSIONATE ROMANCE

Neighbors didn't knock on the door or ring the doorbell. They just came in and hollered.

"Jane, want to talk to you." Wilma lived next door. She sounded a little frantic. It was after dark on a warm summer evening.

Jane had just finished her busy senior year and she was relaxing that summer before going away to the College of William and Mary in Williamsburg, VA. She was lying on the couch in the living room and reading "A Tree Grows in Brooklyn" that Polly had recommended. Jane wanted to teach school and to be a writer. Reading was necessary preparation for both of these plus she had a love affair with books.

Wilma came into the living room and said, "Can we sit on the front porch? I need to talk and sitting in the dark would help."

Jane was barefoot but didn't bother to put on her shoes. She had always loved going barefoot in the house. She also liked to read while in bed or on the couch. Going barefoot and lying down with a good book would remain two of her favorite habits for all of her life.

They sat together on the swing. It was quiet. The only motion that evening was that of the lighting bugs dancing in the moonlight.

"I'm going to have a baby," Wilma blurted out.

Jane didn't know what to say. "Are you sure?"

"Yes, Dr. Irby confirmed it today and he called my mother. She was furious."

Jane was afraid of Wilma's mother when things were going according to normal. She couldn't imagine how little nervous Wilma could deal with this woman whose husband was "henpecked" and everyone "walked on eggs" when she was around.

"Can I give you a shower?"

"I don't think so. Just don't stop being my friend."

"Of course not."

"This means I won't get to finish high school and neither will Bobby Lee. He is getting a job at the factory and we will have to live with Mama and Daddy. I really wanted to ask you how you managed the sex thing when you and T.J. have gone steady for three years?"

Jane didn't want to say the reason was that she didn't want to get pregnant.

"We have a passionate romance. I love him, support him, and trust him but it is without sex. He is my friend. Also he has never asked me to marry him. We, neither one, are very sophisticated. He is very good at kissing and cuddling." She probably didn't want to say that it was a mixture of Biblical fear, not wanting to hurt her mother, wanting to go to college, ambition, optimism, wanting to keep a good reputation. She was fortunate that this wonderful young man made her feel adored and special. All he said about it was he wanted her to be happy and she was happy.

"Have you been very sick?"

"Yes, I really 'toss my cookies' every morning. Bobby Lee and I are getting married. Will you and T.J. come with us? Mama and daddy will sign the papers. Bobby Lee will have to get his parents to sign too. I think we will go to the court house and get the judge to do it. Oh, Jane, remember how we used to plan our weddings.

Bobby Lee is not my knight in shining armor, but he is nice and he is going to marry me. Some fellas just disappear."

With this thought, the two girls spent the evening reminiscing about their childhood. Jane had voted for Wilma's drawing in first grade. They had once corrected each other's spelling tests and given themselves a hundred. That happened to be the last time Jane cheated in school. She had as very irritating conscience. Wilma had not been much of a student and had to repeat third grade even though Jane had "sinned" to help her pass.

In the forties, the only birth control a girl had was a firm "No." Jane was blessed that she didn't have to give sex for love. T.J. was blessed that he had a girl friend who inspired him to get and keep a good reputation. He didn't drink whiskey and even refused to drive a relative's car loaded with "moonshine" though he would have made lots of money. He said years later that he knew Jane would not have liked it. Girls had offered themselves, but he only dated Jane. When she wasn't available, he didn't date anyone.

T.J. was gifted with many of the fruits of the spirit: Galatians 5:22-23. love, joy, peace, patience, kindness, goodness, faithfulness, gentleness, self-control. He said that he didn't set many goals because things fortunately came his way. His faith and character would make him into a leader of men. Meanwhile, Jane was ambitious and wanted to make the world a better place. She wanted to be the woman behind the man. She certainly didn't want to have to push him, but just not get in his way and be there to hold him when the world hurt too much.

The wedding for Wilma and Bobby Lee was the last project that T.J and Jane participated in together.

The vows were said in a sad little chamber with a judge who was in a hurry to get to a trial. T.J. and Jane treated for a wedding dinner of hamburgers and French fries at Frankie Fat's. Jane had Carrie bake a cake and she had placed figures of a bride and groom on top of it, the only symbols from the weddings that she and Wilma had planned. Ray and Peggy had joined them and they all acted happy and sang loudly as they rode home in the familiar blue convertible.

Two weeks later, T.J. boarded a bus and was off to serve his military duty. Korea was now the war to be won. Jane went off to college. It would be 70 years before they were intimate again.

T.J. found his happiness. He needed a structured environment in a Christian atmosphere that could showcase his athletic skills and innate leadership abilities. It was easy for him to follow rules and accept a hierarchy. He was humble. He didn't get in God's way!

Jane remained a helper. She had a more adventurous life if not a peaceful one until she found her joy in her faith. She took risks and created her career instead of accepting "what had been." Her curiosity remained. She finally accepted her need to love and be loved as a God given gift.

CHAPTER 13

THE MAGIC OF THE TOUCH

Jane wrote about the amazing reunion that she and T.J. experienced. God gave them eighteen months of rediscovery. Jane was 85 and T.J. was 86. Both of them had cancer, had lost their spouses and were standing at the doorway to eternity. When they got to heaven, T.J. said he wanted to play the trumpet and Jane bid for the kettle drums. Jane wanted to tell T.J. how he had saved her sanity. He wanted her to know how she set him on the right path for a good life. They agreed that God was the designer in all of this. They had some business to settle, some questions to be answered, and they each wanted to share how those young years of friendship had benefited them.

Jane sent a condolence card to the family when T.J.'s wife died. Later a "proud of you" was sent on the internet when he was honored at the State Capitol. She was three thousand miles away from him and her home state. What she wanted to do was thank him for the wonderful relationship they had shared through three years of going steady in high school.

T.J.'s prostate cancer had metricized in his bones. His health and the loss of a much loved wife of 50 years, had hurled him into a depression. He was looking at some pills that would cut his journey short. He was in a dark place.

Jane's story:

I had lost my only son. I was able to talk about losses. But mainly I listened to my old friend, and as I listened, I discovered he had a wonderful life story. I had published four books as part of my life's work in the field of aging, studied Guided Autobiography at U.S.C and had a master's degree with a concentration in social gerontology. I wanted to write our story.

The story begins in the fall of my freshman year in high school. I had finished with Girl Scouts and Saturday afternoon matinees. He was a sophomore and he had been a Boy Scout, an athlete and involved in church activities. Neither of us had ever dated.

In our small town, attending movies on Saturday night was more exciting than one might imagine. The girls were allowed to go to the movies as a group. The boys weren't far behind. That night someone said "girl boy, girl boy" and I found myself sitting next to a football player I had never met before. Shy, sideways glances were exchanged. I smiled and he took my hand. We never let go as the movie ended and we walked to my house. At the very beginning it felt right, comfortable and safe. Holding his hand made me happy.

In my eighties, I published a poem about that night, 70 years later

Holding hands in High School
You were one of the guys
I was one of the girls
Your hand reached mine
And we never let go
We walked in the rain
We had no car
Courage aCame from love and support

We discovered each other
Seventy years and….
Some memories never die
We can wonder at our blessing
We had cancer and much sorrow
Enjoy today
We can talk tonight

And talk we did. For eighteen months he called at once a day and most often in the AM and PM. He was 3,000 miles away, neither he nor I were internet savvy. Instead of using my tablet, I bought an Apple Smart phone for privacy. His family counted 60+ phone calls to me in one month. We agreed to end our calls if it upset them too much. His children had watched him treat his wife with love and respect. That is often the way children learn to respect their parents. My children were glad to see me so happy. I had not had a date in forty years. My feeling of pure joy had dimmed since my son died. With T.J., I found myself having a real belly laugh. I regained my sense of playfulness. He called from the post office parking lot, from his car, and in the evenings after ten o'clock, seven my time. My friends were delighted to hear about my new life. Most of them talked to him as I handed the phone over to anyone visiting or attending a party at my house. Araceli always talked to him on Tuesday when she came to clean. I wanted him to be included in my life. He wasn't shy, he felt the same way.

Fall in Virginia is all orange, red and yellow. The woods are aglow with color. For us, it meant football, Halloween parties, my birthday celebrated and school of course. There was no clinging to each other in the school halls. Our generation saved the cuddling and kissing for the living room while we listened to our music. The music of the forties had romantic lyrics and "Always" by Irving Berlin was our favorite. "I'll be loving you always, with a love that is true always." As young lovers everywhere we were sure that was true, certainly till the end of the semester. Number 51 was T.J.'s number on the football field and he was wonderful, and my guy!!!

Winter snow was a treat. It painted all the ugliness white. Snow only lasted a day or two. We had snow ice cream, sleigh rides with steep hills, walks with mittens holding gloves and a glorious month of Christmas. We both loved carols and went caroling with our friends. Mama had "open house" on Christmas Eve and everyone was invited…the mailman, all of my friends, older folks, young folks. The egg nog with brandy was on a separate table from the egg nog for the teens or strict Baptist. T.J and I talked about the Christmas tree in the living room. I remembered the soft glow of light from the tree. The mood was mellow until one light went out and the whole row would disappear. T.J. would have to search through the scratchy pine and find the culprit light before the row would light up again.

Spring in Virginia welcomes flowers… daffodils, tulips, and rhododendron while dogwood and laurel decorate the mountainside. We walked in the spring rain but the only time I remember him walking me home from school was in a downpour. I had given him a towel to dry off and he was combing his hair when my mother walked in and was startled to see him. T.J. remembered how scared he was. I said years later, "Aren't you glad you didn't have to tell her I was pregnant?" He agreed that the rules on that subject were the right ones. He would have gone to work in the factory. I would have complained every day that I didn't get to go to college. Mostly spring meant baseball and he was the catcher. He said that being the catcher meant he was in on every play. Once I saw him climb the chicken wire with one hand and catch the ball with the other hand. He said that he could always hear me yelling in the stands. He was captain of the baseball team and he invited his dad to the MVP banquet. After dinner, the coffee was served and his dad poured his coffee into his saucer. T.J. decided to do the same. He didn't want to embarrass his father. He was thoughtful, insightful and compassionate.

Summer meant swimming. We laughed about one trip to Fairy Stone Park when he drove the school football bus. I have no idea why that was allowed since he was seventeen years old. I had on a two piece bathing suite and when I dived into the water, my top came off. T.J. had to rescue me and my top. He said that he never looked. I told my niece about it the other day, "At 86, he would have seen more then than he would now," she said. T.J. and I both laughed at this since we took this aging thing in our stride. We had recent pictures of each other along with high school annual pictures. He said if they gave him one more year with his new treatment, he would be on his knees begging me to marry him. I asked him who was going to pull him up. We laughed so much. Never thought the other person had a subtle meaning in the words spoken. We finished each other's sentences, so comfortable, and at home though we were three thousand miles apart. He said he didn't care what I said, he just liked the sound of my voice. I loved his soft Southern accent. He said it was a marriage of the spirit. We agreed that it was a gift from God. We didn't analyze it, just accepted and were grateful.

T.J. said that he wanted to know everything that had happened to me after I told him I was going to attend proms and experience all of college life. I did just that. There were six boys to every girl so dates for the proms weren't a problem. I joined Kappa Kappa Gamma Sorority and made friends from other parts of the country. The scholastic standards were high; my dorm roommate flunked out my freshman year. I was challenged and would take my alarm clock down to the living room and study all nights when I had a big exam. (study, sleep fifteen minutes and study). I made it into the traveling choir, enjoyed theater class and acting in plays. My lab instructor was a brilliant pre-med student and I dated him for two years. I dated other fellows, mostly veterans who were interested in getting married since they were back from the War and had dreamed of a wife, a house and a dog. I loved the College life. No cars, sexless Monday (no dates), curfews, no boys allowed in the girl's rooms, Honor System, and a heritage to make one proud.

T.J. was a Paratrooper and again Captain of his Army football team. Went in as a private and came out as a sergeant. He could have gone to Officers' Training School but chose to go to college on the G.I. Bill. We agreed that the G.I. Bill was the government's best investment. Many men and women could go to college and earn more money thus pay more taxes and became better citizens. For T.J, it meant a chance to play football and again become the Captain of the college team. After graduation, he became a Coach and a teacher. Many young men were inspired by this good man of character who lived by the morals he taught.

Summer for me meant singing and acting in "The Common Glory" and earning some money while enjoying living away from home with theater people. T.J. came to a production but saw me with Bill Aires, visiting from Washington and Lee. He didn't even let me know he was there. (no communication). One summer, I worked at Marshall Fields in Chicago and lived with my roommate's family. Quite a change from a small mountain town. All this time T.J. played summer baseball for factories who had good competing teams.

When I told T.J. I was taking a fraternity pin, he figured that my "love was dead" and said he really didn't date much for several years until he met his future wife. I waited five years before I got married and that was after much concern. I loved my future husband very much but I was leaving my family, friends, my culture and my beautiful, Virginia. Chicago was like another country.

T.J. married the right woman for him. I married a law student who easily made decision. We started our marriage in a one bedroom apartment on the fourteenth floor of a housing project in

Southside Chicago. We were there three years. We had a future and hope. Most of the other residents didn't have either.

We had three children and had moved to California by the time we joined a legal group to finally practice law and earn a living. We moved again in three years so he could set up a private practice, also in California. Now we had four children under six and my husband had a heart attack. I was in a silent panic…no family nor friends nearby. He recovered and I had a panic attack. I wish I had known what panic attacks were for it really scared me. I became anxious and depressed. I lost weight, I lost myself. My husband and I were both exhausted. I remembered T.J. and our relationship. I found my own voice and it gave me strength and with God's help, the emotional pain lifted and I got well. I told T.J. that he saved my sanity. His response was that he may have saved my sanity but I may have saved his life.

In one of our first conversations, T.J. asked if I were a believer. I had never been asked that before. Once a lady had asked if I were sanctified, for all of their members were. I decided not to join them for I was sure I wasn't good enough for that group. With T.J., I said "I guess so since I am facilitating a Bible study in my home." The next week I got a copy of "Halley's Bible Handbook "in the mail. When my group saw my new resource and heard about T.J.'s health problems, they wanted to know all about him. I introduced them to T.J. and what he meant to me. From then on, he was part of our group. We prayed for him. He talked to each person, if he called when they were there. They shared my roses when he sent two dozen. It was such fun for T.J. and us.

At night, on the phone and Sundays after church, we discussed our faiths. Faith could have clashed over politics. T.J. was a conservative Republican. His daughter had told me that Fox was on every television in the house.

I had changed political allegiances, after my husband had died, and I had voted for President Obama. I had testified before a

Congressional hearing on behalf of older women. (I was in my fifties). I felt that the Fox Channel on television had a malicious and angry tone in their commentators' reviews of the news. T.J. said immediately that politics would not disrupt our relationship! It had taken little for us to be comfortable talking to each other about anything.

T.J. had empathy for others. I had high standards but unfortunately sometimes I had the same expectations for others unless they were handicapped, then I turned into a helper. This helper had much advice, welcomed or not. I wanted to help him with his grief. I remembered the deep sadness of losing a loved one. We talked about the pain of losing someone dear. It was really one of those downhome, take your shoes off, scratch where you itch relationships. I knew he wouldn't hurt me or take what I said in a malicious way. He was better at remembering names than I was and I was surprised at how smart he had gotten. His grammar and spelling were perfect...he had taught English, had an amazing knowledge of history and always read the first and last chapter of a book. After he read "The Road to Character" by David Brooks, he sent it to me and we discovered how our careers had taken parallel roads. He motivated youth to lead structured, disciplined lives dedicated to their faith and country. I taught high school, coordinated a youth program that helped many young people get scholarships. I later taught older adults. Both of us had taught Sunday school, me with high school students, he with adult men. His career was more disciplined, mine more creative. I was a resource person for Senior Centers and nursing homes. Both of us had been successful, with the Lord's help, for we were true believers!!!

Several nights we got around to discussing wars. Now, T.J. didn't seem to know a war that he didn't have some reason for us to be in it and win it. Korean War?? We had curtailed Communism. Vietnam?? We both agreed there should be no demonstrating against war as long as we had soldiers fighting. My favorite nephew had been in Vietnam. The history of that country would make you rethink "going to war." Then I lectured more than he probably wanted to hear. France had Vietnam as a colonial property, Japanese fought the Vietnamese, we fought the Japanese then we fought the Vietnamese. The information I read about the war was that they were killing Catholics and there was a threat for spreading communism. A family from Vietnam had four teens who participated in my nursing home volunteer program. On the wall in my bedroom is a large picture of a rose that their gifted son made for me. He had done the drawings for three of my books. Amazing, I could send T.J. a picture of that rose on my Apple IPhone.

T.J. wanted to be a volunteer and be in the first wave of older soldiers to fight in Afghanistan and Iraq since they would the first killed. We agreed that the war was sure different from "our war." I said that the enemy would just scatter like cock roaches. My idea was that the mothers would be the best way to reach a solution, raise men of honor. He thought that the men would never allow it since the women have no power. I said that they had the power of the kitchen and the bedroom. Also Proverbs mentions how a nagging wife can make life miserable for a husband.

We talked about everything. I told him about the night I had a sleepover with my best friend, Peggy. We were talking late into the night and I told her we could never marry because I would nag him to death by always pushing. I referred to Shakespeare's "Taming of the Shrew". I didn't want to ruin what we had. T.J. had said that all he wanted was to be happy. I wanted to make things better, make my life count for something. That is exactly what T.J. did. He made other people better and also happy. He made me happy!

T.J. made me a better person. I often think now that "It will work itself out" when I have a problem…that excludes internet computer stuff. I remember, as he did, that God is the Commander in Chief. I just trust and listen. I don't have to fix everything. I don't need to express an opinion on everything. T.J. was a listener and I can be too. I can try to lead my life so I lead by good example. Also I learned I was loveable and that I need to take up for myself. I was loved by the one of the best man I have ever known! I can claim it now and I can write it down.

T.J. had thousands of admirers and some close friends. He was thoughtful and sent two dozen roses instead of one dozen so I could share. A neighbor with M.S. called and said, "I hear our friend died." I asked who had died. She said, "You know, the one that sends us roses." I loved that we had friends together.

T.J. was an encourager. His football players knew they were winners so they won the game. I was his favorite writer so I write this story.

It was fun for him to tell me about his football/baseball adventurers since the stories were all new to me, I really enjoyed laughing with him. I wrote a short rhyme about his job as a coach.

Old Coach says:
I like my corn bread hot
And my buttermilk cold
My football tough
The tickets sold
My evenings quiet
And my sweetheart old!
He laughed that the poem was on target.
We became poets as we continued our rediscovery. T.J. said he had never written a poem in his life.
Then he wrote:
To Jane
When I was young and not planning ahead
I lost my first love,

Thinking her feelings were dead
As years went by
We traveled our different ways
The memories were always there of earlier days
Then we met again in our twilight years
And the mature love that emerged
Has brought JOY worthy of tears.

Sometimes I write silly rhymes just for fun. We were both
having trouble with computers:
Smart phones, I pads and a book without a page
Leave me longing for a different age
I'm ten times eight plus an added six
Communicating can leave me in a fix
Like to look 'em in the eye
Know if there is a sigh
Back when manners were kind
Didn't share everything on our mind
Respect for those older
Made them quite a bit bolder
So I'll go out today
And get in somebody's way.

(After shoe shopping and only able to find old lady shoes
that kept my balance}
My Old Shoe
My foot settles into place
Security comes without a lace
There are no blisters to show
Just comfort on the go.
Wish my life was like that!

God Gave Me A Present
Today I can smile or cry
I can laugh or sigh
The sun is out
I can walk about
My friends may call or no one at all
The past is gone
The future unknown
A-h-h-h But
Today is a present!

Older Men
When I am a man very old
I'll be most carefree and bold

I'll have an affair
Even one and a spare
(with worry and care. Baptist version}

I'll eat milk with bread in it
Park etiquette for a minute

It won't always be nice
But I'll love giving advice

And I'll cherish my days
But I won't mind my ways

I'll be so old that no one will care
Except my old friends
Who will all want to share!!

We had so much fun and we wish that everyone would get a God's blessing like we both shared. We were two old people with cancer who cared about each other. T.J. prayed every night that our relationship would be a blessing to our families. He said that his love for me took nothing away for his love for his wife. She was not here now. This happens often when a spouse dies if the couple have had a successful marriage. We certainly never had an affair. After my son had died, I had a sad spot in my heart but with T.J. I was able to feel whole again. I had developed a poor self-image and a deep sadness over failures in life. When T.J. died, I didn't grieve, I was grateful as shown in this poem.

The Magic of the Touch
Their hands chance to touch as they sat side by side
Which the friends who were with them would later confide
The magic of the grip conveyed the feelings
That the young hearts felt
The grip did not slip as they walked to her home
Wishing all along the way they could be alone

The magic of the touch quickly affected the young hearts
And the love they felt went off the charts
After three short years of being so close
Separation came like an evil ghost.
Plans for the future would have to be made
And the magic of the hearts became infinitely grave.

While the memories still linger with love that had grown
Other partners were chosen to build families of their own.
Time marched on as time must do
And the raising of their families occupied their whole view

A lifetime sped by with its lows and its highs
And each was constantly reminded of their duties and ties.

After the partners they had chosen were buried and gone
The two hearts reconnected and they were no longer alone
Long distance conversations were all that was needed
To keep the years from diminishing the power of the feeling
All though the twilight years have taken their toll
They cannot extinguish the love that withstood getting old.

So here's to the first time we ever did love
And here's to the last love this side of the above
The fact that they are the same after seventy years separation
Is a God given miracle that defies explanation!

He called at 1:30 AM his time, during the week he died, and said,
"No matter what happens tonight, I loved you deeply."

Neither of us understood the "why or what" of those eighteen
months. We accepted them as "A Gift of Love."

The End

1946 War Is Over

President Roosevelt is dead and Harry Truman is President. No
Vice President.

U.S. Population is 141,388,866   Unemployment was 3.9%   Life
Expectancy was 62.0 years

U.S. Serviceman Frederick Mellinger starts a lingerie business
featuring European styles. It is shocking but successfully known as
Frederick's of Hollywood!

The bikini swimsuit, named after Bikini Atoll ; the atomic ex-
plosions conducted there, debuts in Paris.

Hasbro introduces Tonka Trucks.

First general –purpose electronic computer, is unveiled in PA.

First drive-up teller windows open in Chicago at the Exchange National Bank.

GIs wanted to buy! New house was $5,600. Incomes average was $2,500 per year. New car was $1,125. The average rent was $65 per month. They paid fifteen cents a gallon for gas and water and oil were checked for free.

Postage was three cents and a movie ticket was fifty-five each. Groceries were reasonable.

Sugar was 75 cents for 10 pounds. Milk was 70 cents a gallon, bacon was 47 cents a pound and add coffee at 50 cents a pound, eggs were 22 cents a dozen and bread was 10 cents a loaf.

Zenith radio played: "My Friend Irma,"—"The Abbott and Costello Show,"—"Life With Luigi,"—"The Fred Allen Show,"— "The Lone Ranger," and "The Goldberg's." Jane and T.J.'s favorite was "Your Hit Parade."

Birthrates jump to over 1.4 million in one year with return of the veterans.

WW II veterans, making use of the provisions of the GI Bill of Rights, head off to college in record numbers.

The Professional Basketball Association of America is formed, elevating the sport to major league status.

St. Louis Cardinal Enos Slaughter scores from 1st base on a double to cinch World Series for the Cardinals. (Giants win 70 years later.)

Philippines gain their full independence from U.S. after 381 years of colonial rule.

The first radar contact with the moon is made by the U.S. Army Signal Corps. The first American-built rocket leaves Earth's atmosphere, reaching an altitude of 50 miles.

Mensa International is formed in Britain for people with high IQs

Ho Chi Minh is elected president of North Vietnam.

Italians turn Italy into a republic from a former monarchy.

Emperor Hirohito of Japan announces he is not a god.

Japanese were trying to reestablish their lives after being interned in camps because they looked like the enemy.

Winston Churchill coins the phrase "Iron Curtain." He also argues for a "United States of Europe."

U.N. holds first General Assembly in London.

The future was bright for us. We had not been bombed and had friendly neighbors to north and south of our borders plus an ocean on both sides. The military forces were back home and ready to go to work. We were poised to be the industrial capital of the world. We had "come of age."

CARRIE'S RECIPES
APPLE COUNTRY RECIPES

Fried Apples

Wash tart apples and slice (with skins on) in thin slices. Fry in bacon fat, covering the pan until apples are tender, then add brown sugar and white sugar to taste. The brown sugar gives the delicious flavor, the white sugar makes apples brown more quickly. Add more grease if necessary.

Stuffed Apples

Core large sound apples, fill the center with chopped figs, nuts and raisins. Add brown sugar allowing two tablespoons for each apple. Place the apple in a deep baking dish, add a little water; bake until tender. Serve with whipped cream.

Or: Filling the apples with 2 cups of mashed sweet potatoes sweeten with sugar and butter.

Apple Pie

Fill unbaked pie shell with 6 apples sliced thin. Mix half teaspoon of cinnamon, 2 tablespoons of lemon juice and a half teaspoon of cinnamon and sprinkle over the apples. Mix half cup brown sugar and half cup of flour and cut in 2 tablespoons of shortening and two tablespoons of butter until mixture is like meal. Add a half cup of pecans. Sprinkle over the apples. 450 oven for 10 minutes and reduce heat to 350 and bake 35-40 minutes.

Apple sauce.
Core as many apples as you need. Stew with sugar and some cinnamon. Add canned apple sauce for stretch and texture. Carrie didn't measuring stuff.

Rob's favorites Chess Pie and Sweet Potato Pecan Pie
For the Chess Pie, Beat 4 eggs and 2 cups of sugar well. Add 1 cup of butter an 2 tablespoons of pure cream. Pour in pastry lined muffin tins and bake in moderate oven. 350 degrees until brown and set. The pastor's wife also made these to be sold at the lunch counter at the drug store.

Sweet Potato Pie: 1 and ½ cups of mashed sweet potatoes. Add 1 teaspoon of cinnamon, ¼ teaspoon salt, ½ cup brown sugar, 1 teaspoon ginger, 2 well beaten eggs and 1 ½ cups of scalded milk. Combine, cool and bake in unbaked pie shell at 350 degrees for 20 minutes until set. Sprinkle with mixture of: ¼ cup butter, 1 cup brown sugar, ¾ cup of chopped pecans. Bake about 45 minutes. Top with whipped cream.

Carrie would use her hand to test the wood stove oven since there was no built in temperature control.

Experience and patience had taught her to be an excellent cook.

Friday's dinner often featured sea food. Often recipes figured you wouldn't eat the fish raw. They didn't do sushi.

Salmon Loaf: 2 cups of salmon, 1 cup crushed corn flakes, 3 eggs, beaten, 1/2 cup of milk. ½ tablespoon of chopped parsley,

1 tablespoon melted butter, ½ teaspoon salt. Combine and put in greased baking dish. Bake in an oven at 350. Recipe didn't say how long????

Baked fish: (any of your choice)
Fry 3 or 4 onions in bacon grease, add little water and cook a few minutes. Salt and pepper to good size fish, put in baking dish with onions and 4 strips of bacon to cover. Bake until well done. Didn't say how long????

Deviled Crab Cakes:
1 lb. crab meat, ¼ cup butter, ½ tsp. black pepper, 2 eggs, 1 tsp. salt, ½ cup bread crumbs, 2 tablespoons flour, 1 teaspoon of Worcestershire sauce. Mix all together, form in small flat cakes and brown in fat ½ inch deep in skillet. Turn once.

Oyster Stew:
1 Pint of oysters, 1 pint of milk 1/3 cup butter salt and pepper to taste. Remove oyster from shell, search for pearl. Strain the juice and heat both until oysters curl. Add scalded milk, butter, salt and pepper. Heat just to boiling point, serve at once.

Fried Oysters:
1 pint of select oysters, 2 beaten eggs with salt and pepper. Dip oyster in egg and then cracker crumbs meal; you aren't through, do it again. Pat into shape and fry in deep boiling fat until brown. Good with slaw.

Virginians like soft shell crabs but the cooking directions are a little gross. Select crabs while still kicking. Turn back pointed ends of shell and remove the "dead men." Remove apron at back of crab and cut out mouth and eyes. Wash and drain. Dip crab in beaten egg and then in flour that has been seasoned with salt and pepper. Can use bread crumbs instead of flour. Fry in deep fat for ten or fifteen minutes. Turn only once. Do not discard the yellow semi-liquid mass in the cooked crab as that is the fat to be eaten.

Fried Shrimp: Peel the shell from the shrimp, leaving the tail on. Remove the skin, take by tail and dip in well beaten egg and then in cracker meal, and fry in hot fat until golden brown.

Other supper dishes:

Spaghetti, only pasta dish Carrie made.
Brown 3 lb. pork neck bones, 1 onion and clove of garlic. Add little water and cook a long time, until onion dissolves. Add two cans tomato sauce, basil and garlic salt. Cook a long time. Take out neck bones, don't bother with making meat balls, throw in 2 lbs. of spicy pork sausage. Cook for one hour.

Chicken soup:
Wash and put whole chicken in water to cover. Add onion, salt and pepper. Remove chicken and cut meat bite size for soup. Add any vegetables in the refrigerator: Corn, carrots, potatoes. Heat all together, add chicken bouillon if need stronger flavor.

Cracklin' Bread:
Cracklings are the pieces of meat remaining after the lard has been rendered from the pork. Mix 2 cups of corn meal, ¼ tsp. salt, ½ soda. Add 1 cup buttermilk, 1 cup of cracklings, diced. Form into oblong cakes and place in greased baking pan. 450 degrees for 30 minutes.

Corn bread:
Beat 2 eggs, add 1 cup thick sour cream, 2 cups of buttermilk and ½ tsp.salt dissolved in the buttermilk. 2 tsp baking powder, 1 tbs. sugar, 3 cups of corn meal. Mix, bake in 400 degrees for ½ hour.

Sweet potato biscuits:
Sift 2 cups flour, ½ tsp. salt, 3 tsp. baking powder. Cut in 4 tbs. of shortening. Stir in sweet potatoes and gradually add ¾ to 1 cup of milk. Cut as desired, cook in 450 to 475 oven. 12 minutes, maybe???

Cranberry Orange Nut Bread:
Chop 1 cup of fresh cranberries. Mix 2 cups flour, 1and 1/2 tsp. baking powder, 1 cup sugar, 1 tsp. salt. Beat 1 egg, grate orange to get 1 tbs. orange peel and ¾ C orange juice Add 2 tbs. shortening. Put in well-greased loaf pan and cook at 350 for 1 hour. Let stand.

Yeast Rolls:
Biscuits were served at breakfast, cornbread at noon dinner and homemade yeast rolls were served at supper time. Dissolve 3 pkgs. of yeast in 2 cups of warm water. Combine 1 cup sugar, 1 cup of Crisco or oil, yeast water and 1 tbs. salt. Add 1 cup scalded milk. Add flour until it is bread dough consistency. Knead until when you poke it, it comes back. Let rise in warm place until it doubles in size. Roll out and cover with butter, cinnamon sugar, brown sugar, nuts, and raisins. It is better if dough is cut into three sections of dough to work with. Roll into jelly roll forms. Let dough rise again. Bake 350 for about 15 minutes. Frost with confectionary sugar frosting made of powdered sugar, vanilla, cream and butter.

Carrot cake:
3 Cups Sugar, 3 whites of eggs unbeaten, 1 ½ tbs. Vegetable oil, beat by hand. Add 2 Cups of flour, 2 tsp. baking soda, 1 tsp. salt, 3 Cups grated carrots, 3 tsp. cinnamon and 2 tsp. vanilla. Cook at 350 for about 20 minutes. Cool. Icing: Cream 1 stick of butter and 1 pkg. cream cheese. Slowly add 1 box of powdered sugar and a cup of pecans.

Pecan Pie

9 inch unbaked pie crust, 1 Cup light corn syrup, 1 Cup brown sugar packed, 3 eggs, 1/3 tsp. salt, 1/3 Cup of butter, 1 tsp. vanilla. Mix and add Cup of pecans. Bake 350-45-50 minutes

Kale:

Wash and put kale in large pot with water to cover. Season with the hunk of salt pork. Cook all morning. Save liquid for Emma to enjoy. She calls it "pot licker".

Made in the USA
San Bernardino, CA
27 January 2017